MOONSHINE & MENACE

MOONSHINE HOLLOW #5

KATHLEEN BROOKS

❀ Created with Vellum

Bluegrass Series

Bluegrass State of Mind

Risky Shot

Dead Heat

Bluegrass Brothers

Bluegrass Undercover

Rising Storm

Secret Santa: A Bluegrass Series Novella

Acquiring Trouble

Relentless Pursuit

Secrets Collide

Final Vow

Bluegrass Singles

All Hung Up

Bluegrass Dawn

The Perfect Gift

The Keeneston Roses

Forever Bluegrass Series

Forever Entangled

Forever Hidden

Forever Betrayed

Forever Driven

Forever Secret

Forever Surprised

Forever Concealed

Forever Devoted

Forever Hunted

Forever Guarded

Forever Notorious

Forever Ventured

Forever Freed

Forever Saved

Forever Bold

Forever Thrown

Forever Lies (coming Jan/Feb 2022)

Shadows Landing Series

Saving Shadows

Sunken Shadows

Lasting Shadows

Fierce Shadows

Broken Shadows

Framed Shadows

Endless Shadows

Fading Shadows (coming April/May 2022)

Women of Power Series

Chosen for Power

Built for Power

Fashioned for Power

Destined for Power

Web of Lies Series

Whispered Lies

Rogue Lies

Shattered Lies

Moonshine Hollow Series

Moonshine & Murder

Moonshine & Malice

Moonshine & Mayhem

Moonshine & Mischief

Moonshine & Menace

Moonshine & Masquerades (coming Dec 2021)

1

Zoey found these quiet times on the dark side of the morning peaceful. She used the time to bake, meditate, and let magic freely flow in and around her. This was her time to reflect on the past, be present for the now, and to prepare for the future.

It had been almost a year since Grand Master Linus had been killed and her father, Magnus Rode, elected the new grand master of the Tenebris. It had been almost a year since she felt the shift in magic when she had killed Ian, the Tenebris Hunter who had helped lead the war against the witches with his leader, Alexander. They'd all heard the cry of fury when Zoey killed Ian and survived the resulting tsunami of blood. Her father had felt the shift too.

However, life had moved on since then. It had been almost a year, but it felt like a lifetime. Witches were happy to be back together and the impending doom Zoey and her father felt was pushed a little farther back in their minds with each day that passed.

Time changed things. Just two years ago, Zoey was a normal woman in Los Angeles. She was a junior associate at a large entertainment law firm working her way toward senior partner. Until one night her action star client got high on drugs, leapt on stage in a strip club, and became the center of an epic battle between his escorts and the club's dancers. Zoey had vaulted to the stage to try to get him out of the club before the police arrived to save his job from being terminated under the morals clause. Too bad that neither the strippers nor the escorts seemed to appreciate her efforts. Long story short, Zoey was arrested as a prostitute and fired from her job. Slade, the club's bouncer, bailed her out of jail and convinced her to let fate decide her next move.

Fate had a sense of humor, that's for sure. Fate sent her to Moonshine Hollow, Tennessee and into a new career as the small town's baker. Fate led her home one night when she saw Vilma and Agnes, who were like grandmothers to her in the new town, being attacked by blasts of light emanating from a very scary dude. Zoey tried to run to their rescue, but she tripped, screamed, and accidently ingested the powers of the Tenebris hunter who had been trying to kill Agnes and Vilma in order to steal their powers. The magical powers of the male witch triggered Zoey's heretofore unknown, and long-hidden, powers inherited from her Tenebris witch father, Magnus.

Fate still wasn't done with her. She'd accidentally become a witch and, as fate would have it, she was now the most powerful witch with powers not seen since the Goddess herself. The female witches, the Claritase, took her in and told her of the war between themselves and the Tenebris Hunters, male witches who had turned bad to gain more power. Then for fun, fate sent Slade back into her life after she'd learned the meaning of the mark of the Tenebris on his neck. Zoey didn't know if Slade was there to kill her or not, but her heart knew the answer. Led by Slade, the True Tenebris, male witches who wanted to do good in the world, and the Claritase joined to fight the Tenebris Hunters together.

Zoey fought in the war and almost lost her life, but together with Slade and their friends, they'd defeated evil. Or so they'd thought. That night last year with Ian, one-time second-in-command of the Tenebris Hunters, and the mysterious voice that caused the blood rain to fall, made Zoey realize the battle between good and evil wasn't over yet.

So every morning Zoey came to her bakery and let her powers tell her if they were safe for another day. Zoey turned on the mixer for the cranberry muffin batter and let the soothing rhythmic sound relax her. She closed her eyes, pulled the magic from her heart, and sent the pureness of it out into the world. She did this every morning when she was alone. It was her way to protect the town that had grown so much over the past year.

She saw the white light from her fifth element power float off into the air. She felt when it reached the homes of the people just now waking for the day. She felt the birds, deer, and critters that filled the woods and mountains surrounding Moonshine Hollow. Finally, Zoey took a deep breath and let the good thoughts of protection and love loose over the town. All was safe for the day.

People streamed into the bakery the second Zoey flipped the open sign and unlocked the door. Some human. Some not. After Zoey and Slade defeated the evil Alexander, Grand Mistress Lauren of the Claritase and the late Grand Master Linus of the Tenebris had sent out word that

Moonshine Hollow was a safe place for all witches, Claritase and Tenebris alike. It was the first time in four hundred years that the witches were living, working, and falling in love together.

Zoey and Slade's wedding had been the first since the war began. She still couldn't believe they'd been married nine months now. While she was full of worry about the unknown threat, she felt, for the first time since the night Ian had died, her life was also filled with love and more happiness than Zoey could ever imagine.

"I felt you searching again," Agnes said as she came to the counter and ordered a muffin.

"Just making sure all is well. And it is," Zoey smiled at the old witch who had become a grandmother to her since arriving in Moonshine Hollow.

"You're worried it might not be one day, though," Agnes's sister Vilma stated. "You might be able to fool all of them— even Grand Mistress Lauren—but you can't fool us."

Zoey glanced at the line of humans and witches waiting for breakfast. The humans had no idea the people standing among them had powers, but humans and witches alike loved one thing–gossip. Zoey nodded to Vilma. "We'll discuss it later."

"No need. We know. We saw the blood. We saw Linus die. Ian wasn't powerful enough to do that. Just remember, we're here if you need us. We've seen you and your father practicing in the woods deep into the night. We might finally be showing our age after a millennium or two, but we still have our powers," Agnes whispered.

"Now, the most important question," Vilma said a litter louder. "What kind of cake are you making for the wedding this weekend?"

The bakery went quiet as everyone leaned forward.

"Italian wedding cake for the bridal cake and a chocolate salted caramel for the groom's cake."

Noise exploded as Vilma winked at her, took her breakfast, and moved to one of the smaller tables in the bakery to eat. The humans had been generous in welcoming the witches. They knew they were friends and family of the core group of witches who had moved in first–Vilma, Agnes, Grand Mistress Lauren, Zoey, Slade, Polly, and Samuel. Polly was Zoey's best witch friend and Samuel was Slade's partner at the sheriff's department and best Tenebris friend. Slowly the rest of the Tenebris and Claritase council were welcomed and over the past six months, a good percentage of witches had either moved or visited the town. They'd also moved into the surrounding mountain towns.

Also exciting was that the Claritase and Tenebris were using their powers as intended once again. It had been four hundred years since they'd been the healers the Goddess had intended. Their role had been to help humans, but the witch war had sent them into hiding. Now they were doctors, therapists, teachers, nurses, and more. They were integrating back into the human world while using their powers. Not that the humans realized it.

"I can't wait to try your cake. This will be the first wedding I've been to since moving here," Clara said with excitement. Clara had moved to Moonshine Hollow eight months ago to open a small boutique store called Moonshine and Pearls. The women had gone nuts over it. Up until then, they all had to buy their clothes online, drive to a bigger town, or make do with what they could get at the hunting store. Zoey had liked her instantly. She was kind, outgoing, had great clothes, and fit right in. Clara had told them that her momma had been from Moonshine Hollow but left when she'd turned eighteen. A story that was very common in small towns. After Clara's mother passed, she'd decided to come to Moonshine Hollow to feel closer to her.

"You are going to love it," Maribelle said. "We've had such an uptick in weddings. It's been so fun. Speaking of weddings and married couples, have you heard from Jane and Galen?" Maribelle was Zoey's first friend she had when she moved to Moonshine Hollow. Maribelle was human, but that didn't stop their friendship from developing into sisterly love.

"They are happy in Scotland. They're going to come visit this summer. I can't wait to see them," Zoey said with a smile. Zoey and Slade regularly *poofed* over to the standing stones to visit the stone keeper and his wife. However, instant magical travel wasn't something she could talk to Maribelle about.

"Now, if only the good doctor could get his wife pregnant," Grand Mistress Lauren grumbled behind Maribelle. "Speaking of pregnant." Grand Mistress Lauren pinned Zoey with a glare. While Zoey and Slade's wedding opened the door to a flood of witch marriages, the little witchlings that everyone were looking forward to welcoming hadn't arrived yet.

"I'm not pregnant. I'm not trying to get pregnant. Get pregnant yourself if you want a baby so badly," Zoey joked back. Only after six months of listening to every witch and human alike asking her every day if she was pregnant yet, it wasn't so much of a joke anymore. In reality Zoey wanted to scream.

"What's this about my little girl being pregnant?"

Maribelle laughed and Zoey groaned. "Dad. I'm not pregnant. Give it a rest."

"Oh, Lauren, can you imagine a little Zoey and Slade boy?" Her father sighed happily.

"You mean a little girl," Lauren corrected and soon Agnes, Vilma, Maribelle and most of the town were in a debate over the gender of a nonexistent baby.

While it infuriated her, it also warmed her heart. These people all loved her, Slade, and their future children. That kind of love was worth fighting for.

2

Slade ducked the punch and followed up with a hook. His fist connected with Samuel's face and sent his Tenebris brother stumbling back.

"I thought this was practice," Samuel grumbled as he rubbed his chin.

"It is. Since there is literally nothing going on in this town in terms of needing to fight, we have to practice harder than ever to stay ready," Slade explained. Slade was the sheriff of Moonshine Hollow and Samuel his deputy. Slade had been able to stay in fighting shape when he was the bouncer at the strip club. He was amazed at how many fights he'd been involved in there. But in Moonshine Hollow? The most he got was a drunken hunter who might give him a little shove, but they'd look up at him and instantly back down.

"Zoey still thinks trouble is coming?" Samuel asked as they got back to sparring.

"Didn't you feel her this morning?"

"I did. I don't have to set an alarm any more. Her magic

wakes me up like clockwork. But she hasn't found anything, right?"

"All is quiet, well except for the Irises and Opossums getting into it over which club should get their cookie delivery first," Slade said with a chuckle. "It's bad when the most trouble in town comes from the old married couples."

"You're in that group now," Samuel pointed out.

"I believe you have to be married twenty years or more to be in the men's only Opossum club or the women's only Iris club. Got a couple decades to go. You, on the other hand," Slade said before delivering a hard right cross, "need to get your butt in gear or you're going to lose your True Love."

"I don't have a True Love," Samuel said, his eyes giving away the lie. Samuel's past involved a broken heart. But however much he trusted his life to Slade, he hadn't yet shared that secret with him.

"You're too scared to find out if Polly is your True Love. You can step in here and practice with me but you can't ask sweet-as-pie Polly out on a date?" Slade followed up the cross with a jab and some *bawks* like a chicken.

"I'll ask Polly out when you have a little witchling," Samuel said, now going on the attack. Slade felt the frustration his wife was feeling at that exact moment. It hit him hard just as Samuel landed a punch. He and Zoey were True Loves. Their magic was intertwined and he could feel what she was feeling and vice versa. He knew it was hard for her to deal with the constant questions of becoming pregnant. Now that they had been married for almost a year people had started asking him too. He felt her frustration mix with his and leveled a punch at Samuel. It sent the man flying and landing hard ten feet away.

"Sorry. If you can't tell, we're a little frustrated with

people asking. It's none of their business when we have witchlings." Slade held out his hand and helped Samuel up.

"I shouldn't have joked about it," Samuel said as a way of apologizing. "Seriously though, you can talk to me if you need to."

"Zoey wants to wait. She says she's having dreams of a dark future. She doesn't want to bring a witchling into that. However, you can have love with Polly," Slade said jokingly. Samuel narrowed his eyes at him and Slade held up his hands. "Fine, that's the last thing I'll say on the subject. Now, let's meet everyone for practice."

Grand Master Magnus, Slade's father-in-law, had initiated the thrice weekly magical workouts. All Tenebris and Claritase worked out together as they grew their powers, worked on defending themselves and each other, and prepared for a day Slade hoped would never come.

Zoey gave her final instructions to the part-time helper she now had for after the morning rush and before lunch. Amelia was a human teenager who was saving for college. She worked four hours every morning to free Zoey up to practice her powers. Not that Amelia knew that.

"Ready to go?" Polly asked as she waited by the front door.

"Have fun at Zumba," Amelia called out. Polly hid her little smirk as Zoey grabbed her purse and joined her on the short hike into the woods where all the witches gathered to practice.

Grand Mistress Lauren cast a protective spell on the area so even if humans wandered by they couldn't see into the clearing where Tenebris and Claritase were zapping things with their elemental powers.

"How many people asked if you were pregnant today?" Polly asked kindly. Polly had never asked Zoey about a baby. She knew why Zoey was waiting.

"*All* of them," Zoey signed. "Tell me something happy. Did Samuel ask you out? You thought he was getting closer."

Polly shook her head and her long ponytail swayed. "No. I'm beginning to think it's not going to happen. I would have sworn he was my True Love, but nothing. Did you see the Cavallaro brothers arrived yesterday?"

"Yes, you can't miss all eight of them. The town couldn't stop talking about them after they found out I am not pregnant again today," Zoey said as they walked farther into Earnest Park.

"Surely one of them would date me," Polly said with a sigh. Polly and Samuel had been flirting since they'd first been brought together in Moonshine Hollow. Every time it seemed they'd made some progress, Samuel would back off.

"But none of the Cavallaro brothers are your True Love," Zoey said gently. She was going to have to have a word with Samuel. It was one thing to not be interested, but he regularly showed real interest in Polly. He was always there to open the door for her, to ask how her day was, to be her partner in powers practice. Something deeper was going on and Zoey was going to find out what it was.

Polly sighed and shook her head. "They're not. I've waited over four hundred years. I've walked through fire, literally, and I'm tired of waiting. Many witches don't find their True Loves but can still be happy. I just need to accept it. Samuel doesn't want me. I need to move on."

Zoey felt the power of the shield as they approached the

clearing. All looked well, but even so, Zoey closed her eyes and sent out her powers just to make sure.

"You know that wakes everyone up every morning, right? I haven't slept in for nine months."

Zoey called back her powers in surprise and grimaced. "Oops. Sorry."

"It's okay. We all know you're just trying to protect us. Maybe just wait until seven to search the woods? Five is a little early and some of the new witches who didn't go through what we have don't understand why you're doing it. We've explained, but it would go a long way at keeping the peace to wait an hour or two. Too many tired witches mixed with magical powers during practice can be a little dangerous."

Zoey nodded and as much as she wanted to have it not matter, it did. She just wanted to keep everyone safe. It fell to her. She'd seen it. She knew there was something darker out there. She and Slade were the protectors and had the responsibility of protecting every witch here. However, everyone else only cared about sleeping in and whether or not she was pregnant. It was so frustrating. Zoey wanted to scream, but instead she walked into the clearing with a smile plastered on her face.

Slade was waiting for her with Samuel by his side. Zoey instantly calmed when Slade took her hand in his. "Samuel, would you take Polly to the armory and begin setting things up?" Slade phrased it like a question, but it was an order—one Samuel and Polly immediately followed. "What's the matter, sweetness?"

"Everyone is growing complacent. Samuel is dragging his feet and about to lose his chance at True Love. Everyone is bugging me about becoming pregnant. And while I am so happy and madly in love with you, I have this feeling that something bad is going to happen and it's growing stronger every day."

Slade bent and covered her lips with his. The kiss was gentle and full of compassion that warmed her heart and sent the bad thoughts scurrying for cover. "Better?" Slade asked as he cupped her cheek with his large hand.

"Yes, let's practice."

Zoey knew Slade could feel that she had lied. The kiss had calmed her and was just what she needed, but the feeling of dread came storming back the second his lips left hers.

3

Polly may be sweet as pie, but not when it came to fighting. She was every inch a warrior. She'd had to be to survive so many centuries. She'd been born in Europe but her family moved to North America on the first voyage to Roanoke Island in 1585, when she was not even a hundred years old. What happened there wasn't her story to tell. What she could tell was it was where she learned to fight and to heal. She'd watched the colonies grow as she moved around from settlement to settlement, helping and healing anyone who needed it, until Alexander fooled them all into coming to Tenebris headquarters.

There, as just a young witch, she'd worn the fashion of the times–a large court dress. It was heavily adorned with bright silk embroidered in floral patterns with pearls as the center of the flowers. The lace at her neck and sleeves was so delicate she was afraid to touch it. However, the lessons learned in the wilderness of the American Colonies were strapped to each calf. She might be a healer, but Polly knew full well that threats to women came from every direction.

Her fire power had simmered in her belly, the knives on her calves warmed under the energy as she and her parents stood in court, waiting for Alexander to speak. Since Alexander had been named Grand Master, the two groups of witches had never been more divided. Recently there were rumors of the Tenebris and Claritase coming together more.

That didn't happen. Instead Alexander killed Grand Mistress Helena in front of them all as all hell broke loose. The Tenebris had turned on the Claritase. The fighting, the screaming, the pain . . . it was all still in her nightmares. That night everything had changed. The Tenebris had split between those who followed Alexander's ideas of stealing powers to create a strong leadership and killing off any competition, to those who followed the beliefs of the Goddess.

Polly hadn't frozen when the fighting started like so many of her friends had. She'd been in the wilderness for years, honing her reflexes and skills. Her fire power surged from the fingertips of her left hand as she hauled up the large dress and pulled a knife with her right. Blood poured from any Tenebris Hunter who approached her as she battled her way toward Alexander and his men.

"Save the council!" her mother had yelled in the midst of her own battle. It was the last time Polly had seen her parents.

Lauren had shape-shifted into a black cat to try to sneak up on Alexander when he turned on her. His powers had rained down on Lauren, stripping her of hers, and trapping her in the form of her cat until Grand Master Linus freed her only recently. Neferu, one of the oldest witches in the Claritase, was using her air power to drive Alexander back and protect her best friend, Lauren.

Agnes and Vilma, who appeared to be in their fifties at the time, had joined in the battle to protect the council.

Zap, zap, stab. Polly was covered in witches' blood as she fought her way to the council members. Some were dead or dying and couldn't be saved. But Neferu, Lauren, Vilma, Agnes, and a few others were still alive. They needed to find the witch preventing teleportation and kill him. Then Polly could get her sisters to safety.

"Watch out!" a deep voice had boomed next to her.

Polly instantly ducked as a flash of air power shot over her head. Polly jammed the knife upward and into the heart of the Hunter who'd had tried to attack her. When Polly looked to see who had warned her, she found a young man fighting by her side. Tall, with a neatly trimmed dark beard, and so very muscled that he reminded her of a knight. He nodded at her and she nodded back, and then they both turned their attention back to the battle, taking down Hunter after Hunter.

No one knew which powerful witch had cast the spell preventing teleportation, but at some point, they must have died because suddenly the power-like bubble keeping them trapped vanished. In a split-second, the cavernous court was empty of the living. Polly transported back to the colonies, alone. The Claritase book chimed with an update urging all Claritase into hiding. For four hundred years, Polly hid in the remote wilderness of the southern colonies, that eventually became states, with little more than a dream of the man who had warned her as her company. Until one night, a little over a year ago, Grand Mistress Lauren had appeared in her living room.

"My faithful warrior. The time has come. The prophecy is at hand and we need your help."

Polly fit right in to Moonshine Hollow. It was like the

numerous towns she moved to every ten years all through the southern United States. But now she was no longer alone, Polly had friends and that was worth fighting for. Then one day she'd met Slade and the True Tenebris had joined their fight.

When Slade's second-in-command stepped forward, Polly had almost fallen down from the shock. It was the man who had fought by her side. The one she'd dreamed about for four hundred years.

And now, here he was in front of her again. Yet, the warrior she knew to be just as brave as her wouldn't ask her out. Was it only her? Four hundred years was a long time to dream about someone. Maybe she'd turned their brief encounter on the battlefield into something more than it was.

Well, maybe Samuel just needed to fight for her because she was tired of trying to fight for him.

"Samuel," Polly said as they set up for practice. He turned and his eyes met hers in a way that sent a shock to her heart and a flutter to her stomach. "Which Cavallaro brother is that?" She pointed at random at the herd of large Italian Tenebris witches currently surrounded by a flock of Claritase witches.

"Why?" Samuel asked as his jaw twitched.

"Because, I'm tired of waiting for you to make a move, and he seems to know which move to make," Polly said sweetly as she smiled at the muscle bound Cavallaro man. No matter how they preened, they still weren't Samuel. She just didn't need to tell Samuel that. "So, which one is that?"

"They're no good for you. They're broom bunnies. They're only after one thing when it comes to witches. To see how many they can get in bed," Samuel bit out with frustration.

"Maybe this witch needs a little sweeping off her feet. A broom bunny will do the job." Polly set down the table they were moving and walked off. She prayed he'd come after her, since she was done chasing after him.

Samuel watched the love of his life walking away and felt like killing someone. But he couldn't love her. It wasn't possible. He'd already found his True Love.

"Where's Polly?" Zoey asked as she and Slade joined him as he laid out the weapons the witches could use for practice. They weren't weapons like guns and knives, but magical weapons—spells, items that could be used to enhance or channel powers, and such.

"I'm not her keeper," Samuel snapped before he heard Slade growl in displeasure.

"I'm sorry, Samuel. I didn't mean—" Zoey reached out and touched his arm and suddenly Samuel was back at the Tenebris court, four hundred years ago. The battle was raging all around him.

Samuel was there, but he wasn't. He saw his past self fighting, and as he looked down, he saw Zoey still clasping his hand. However, the sounds, the smells, and the horror were all very real.

"Katrina!" Samuel heard his past self yell. Samuel tracked his voice to see the Tenebris Hunter stealing the last of his wife's life from her body. They had only been married two months. They were young to be married, and while the True Love bond hadn't formed all the way, there were the beginnings of it. He knew in only a short time the True Love bond would be complete.

Samuel saw himself run to his bride. His sword swung

taking the head of the Tenebris Hunter who had taken Katrina's powers clean off. "Kat, can you hear me?"

The past Samuel dropped to his knees and cradled Katrina's head in his arms. "True Love," she said in shallow gasps. "She's here."

"Yes, love. You're still here. Stay with me." Samuel remembered that he'd tried to teleport but couldn't. Someone powerful was blocking their ability to retreat. It was a slaughter. "Katrina?"

Samuel watched as his past self shook Katrina, but knew it was no use. His love was gone. A second later her body disappeared. With rage unlike anything he'd felt, he cut through the Tenebris Hunters. Samuel watched his past self lose all control of his powers. Anger fed him as he slaughtered everyone in his path toward Alexander.

Then there she was—Polly. Samuel watched his past self fight not toward Alexander, but toward Polly. He hadn't realized who she was then. He'd never known her name until Slade had introduced them last year in Moonshine Hollow. The past Samuel had fought toward her and then there she was—the fierce warrior who looked too beautiful to be in the middle of a battle.

She's here. Samuel looked around at the voice of Katrina that seemed to take over the memory he was reliving. That was new. That hadn't happened in the past. He looked back down at himself fighting by Polly's side. Zoey removed her hand and they were back in the clearing in Moonshine Hollow.

"What was that?" Slade asked. "I said your name like ten times and no one responded."

Samuel looked down at Zoey, who was now looking at Polly with new admiration. Then he looked at Polly talking to the Cavallaro brothers. *She's here.*

"Did you hear that?" Samuel asked Zoey.

"Hear what?" Slade asked, growing impatient with the lack of answers coming his way.

"I did. I think we both know what it means," Zoey said quietly. Samuel noticed she didn't reach for him again. Instead, she kept her hands clasped in front of her.

"It couldn't. Katrina and I—"

"Were *in love*, but not True Loves. She knew that. Katrina is telling you that you need your True Love by your side for the battle to come. It's no mistake the Goddess and Katrina showed us that particular moment in time," Zoey said as gently as she could, but there was no mistaking the surety in her voice.

"I can't. It would be disrespectful to Katrina's memory," Samuel said just as quietly as Zoey had been talking.

Zoey went to reach for him, but stopped and pulled her hand back. "Samuel, it was a message from Katrina to claim your True Love. She knew it that night. She'd felt Polly and your connection before you did. You still haven't figured it out, have you? The way you fought to reach Polly in a castle full of people. It was Polly you fought side by side with that day. She's your True Love and Katrina came back to tell you so you don't lose Polly, which you are very close to doing."

"Who is Katrina? What happened?" Slade asked again. Zoey reached out and took Slade's hand in his to quiet him.

Samuel didn't answer though. He kept his eyes on Polly. He always did. He always knew where she was, how she was feeling, but he'd tried to convince himself that it couldn't be True Love. Was Zoey right? Katrina and he had loved each other, very much, but there was no bonding like between Zoey and Slade or Jane and Galen. *She's here.* Katrina's voice filled his head once again. Okay, Katrina, message received. Samuel smiled to his first love's voice that practically screamed into his head so loudly that Zoey flinched.

"I think she's being very clear on the matter. You have her blessing. Go, Samuel. Go now or lose her forever," Zoey said, unconsciously reaching for him. She touched his arm again and instantly they were transported, but not to the past. This time it was to the future.

"What in the Goddess's name is going on?" Slade muttered. The three of them stood on top of Earnest Mountain and looked down on Moonshine Hollow. It was burning to the ground. Screams of terror and pain echoed off the mountains and seemed to fill the clouds.

Below them, on the same bridge where Ian had been killed, stood Zoey, Slade, Polly, Samuel, Jane, and Galen. They were surrounded by dark shadows on each side of the bridge that were converging on them as blood rained down.

Darkness was almost upon them when light glowed from above.

"Mom?" Slade whispered.

"Linus!" Samuel gasped, but he noticed Zoey was quiet.

"A traitor, a love taken, families destroyed all for power. A masquerade hiding evil has been in place too long. It's time to reveal who is under the mask. Only a power stronger than True Love can defeat the dark magic as evil as this," Helena said as she looked at her son and daughter-in-law.

"Only together can you stop it. Fate has played her last hand," Linus said with a soft smile.

Helena smiled down at them and blew them a kiss. Linus gave an encouraging smile and then they were gone.

Samuel blinked and there they stood in the clearing, hand in hand. Slade, Zoey, and he saw that his right hand was outstretched toward Polly. He took a deep breath as they all came to terms with the prophecy.

"Excuse me. I have a True Love I need to claim." Samuel dropped his hand from Zoey and stalked across the clearing. First Katrina and then Helena and Linus. The Goddess wasn't just giving hints. She was bashing him over the head to make sure he saw what had been right in front of him for centuries. His real True Love.

4

Polly laughed at something Cavallaro brother number who-knows-what said. She could barely understand his accent, but it was sexy as all get out. However, as if by their own accord, her eyes kept drifting back to Samuel.

It was strange when she had seen Zoey holding on to his arm, but then it was even stranger when Slade, Zoey, and Samuel were standing completely still holding hands, staring off in the distance. Polly glanced over at them now only to find Samuel stalking toward her with a look on his face she hadn't seen since they battled side by side four hundred years ago. His eyes were narrowed, magical power rolled off him, and he seemed impossibly big as he blocked out the morning light.

The brothers said something in Italian, but Polly didn't realize there were other people around them. She saw it, the magical bond beginning to connect them. They *were* True Loves! She gasped as her magic reached for his across the clearing. His reached for hers and together their powers intertwined. Her red fire power licked its way along his green earth power until a yellow light joined them heart to heart.

When Polly looked up from the light Samuel was standing in front of her. "It's been you all along, all this time. The battle at court . . ." Samuel shook his head. "I didn't see it–the way I fought to get to you. I should have. I'm sorry. But I see you now. I see *us*. Four hundred years I've waited to do this."

Polly's heart was beating as she looked up into Samuel's deep brown eyes. "Do what?"

"Kiss you."

Samuel lowered his head and Polly forgot to breathe. When his lips claimed hers, she didn't need air to survive. She had her True Love. Warmth filled her body as their powers crackled around them. Samuel's arm caressed her back as it pulled her tightly against him while his other hand cupped her face to angle her lips just the right way to deepen the kiss. Polly's fingers speared his hair as she tugged him closer.

She didn't know how long they kissed, but she gasped when she finally pulled back. "Samuel, your eyes!" No longer dark brown, his eyes were an amber color glowing back down at her.

"I'd always loved your russet eyes, but this is my favorite color now. We match."

Polly reached up and touched her face. Her whole body seemed to be vibrating with a new energy. "My eyes are amber too?"

"Even more beautiful than gold." Samuel used a finger to push back a lock of hair and then kissed her again. "Let's get out of here."

It was then Polly remembered the entire witch population of Moonshine Hollow surrounded them. Polly looked around only to see white. It was like they were inside an egg.

"Zoey," they said together and then laughed.

Samuel knocked on the wall and the egg disappeared. Around them, witches were working on their powers and Grand Mistress Lauren was smiling, her wedding book in hand.

"I knew you two were True Loves! Two of our greatest warriors were destined to be together." Lauren sighed happily as everyone stopped to notice the new couple. "Now, about the wed—"

Grand Mistress didn't get a chance to finish. Samuel had *poofed* them away.

"No offense to the Grand Mistress, but I'd always imagined being the one to propose to you," he said to a startled Polly.

Polly looked around and smiled when she realized where they were. They were at the Standing Stones of Stenness. It was the place where countless witches had come through the ages for a blessing from the Goddess. It was also the place where their friends, Jane and Galen, now lived as the keeper of the stones.

Polly looked around at the ancient stones in the full Scottish daylight. Down the path sat the stone house where Jane and Galen lived. "I want to get the Goddess's blessing," Samuel said to her.

"I've waited so long for you. I've loved you in my heart for four hundred years," Polly said, reaching out to clasp both of his hands in hers. "But I'm glad we're doing this the traditional way. It means a lot to me, Samuel. I was young when the war started. I lost my parents and our traditions make me feel closer to them."

Samuel bent his head until their forehead rested

together. "Now that I've opened my heart, it's filled with nothing but my love for you."

They closed their eyes and held each other's hands. Samuel spoke softly in the old language of the Goddess. Polly listened as he offered up a prayer to the Goddess, told her of their love, and asked for her blessing. The stones seemed to hum around them as Polly's powers surged to life. They shot from her body and she opened her eyes fearful she'd hurt Samuel. Instead, she found their powers twisting together into one, forming a circle around the stones. Their powers twisted, turned, and combined into a bright yellow light that filled the stones before racing back into their bodies.

Polly gasped at the power she felt flowing through her. It was the power of light, the power of good, the power of love. Zoey had told her that True Loves shared stronger powers, but now she fully understood.

"Congratulations!"

Samuel and Polly looked to the side of the stones to find Jane and Galen smiling at them.

"I knew you'd come to your senses eventually," Galen said to Samuel. "I was afraid I was going to have to give you the True Love talk Slade gave me."

"We have the blessing of the Goddess, now we need the blessing of the stone keepers," Samuel said as he shook Galen's hand and Polly hugged Jane.

"Well you have it. You've had it the whole time," Jane said with a laugh. "Come into the house. Zoey and Slade will be here soon."

"That's nice that they're here to celebrate," Polly said, leaning her head against Samuel's shoulder.

"Tonight we celebrate," Samuel said in a tone that made

Polly look up at him. She noticed the warning in his gaze and wondered what it was about.

"Of course," Jane said, understanding his tone, as she led the way to the house. "We have a cute guest cottage down the path there that you two can use for the night. Tomorrow is soon enough to come back to reality. Now tell me, has Grand Mistress Lauren brought out the wedding book yet?"

Polly wanted to ask more, but Jane shut it down, locked it, and tossed away the key. She was firmly in the pretend there's nothing to talk about tomorrow camp. By the time they arrived to the house, Slade and Zoey were inside popping the cork on a bottle of champagne.

Polly rushed to her best friend's open arms and they hugged.

"I am so happy for you both," Zoey said as she hugged Polly tight.

"I am too. I can't even describe it."

"Nice eyes," Slade said, wrapping Polly up in a bear hug as Zoey smiled at Samuel. "I thought they'd be neon yellow, so that's a relief."

Polly smacked Slade and they laughed as Galen poured the champagne.

"To love and friendship," Samuel said, raising his glass.

They clinked their glasses and took a sip. "You know," Zoey said with a little grimace, "I don't mean to sound like Lauren, but tomorrow is the Autumnal Equinox."

"I was going to say the same thing," Jane said with a laugh. "I've been having dreams. The balance of power between good and evil is off. The Autumnal Equinox symbolizes balance. The day and night are almost equal in duration. I have a feeling it's meant to be this way."

"Excuse me for a moment," Samuel said as he stepped back from Polly and *poofed* away.

"Y'all! It took him four hundred years to realize I'm his True Love and now you've scared him. And what's wrong with waiting a bit to plan a lovely wedding?" Polly would have been angrier, but she still felt Samuel in her heart. He hadn't left her. At least he hadn't withdrawn his love.

"We wanted to wait to tell you until tomorrow, but maybe we should tell you tonight," Jane said as she looked to Zoey.

"Tell me what?" Polly asked. She didn't know why but she was filled with dread.

"It'll be easier if I show you." Zoey reached out and touched her. Blood, screams, terror. They stood on the bridge in Moonshine Hollow fighting a darkness so evil that Polly could still feel it when Zoey let go of her arm.

"Together then," Polly said finally. "Three True Loves bound by love and friendship."

Samuel popped back into the room with a look that could kill. "You told her. I could feel her distress."

"I'm sorry," Zoey said to Samuel, who looked ready to fight anyone for causing Polly distress.

Polly reached out and took Samuel's hand. "I needed to be told. We have tonight. Tell Lauren to plan the wedding for tomorrow at sunset, the exact time that day and night will be balanced."

Polly took a deep breath and felt the rightness of it all. "To tonight. To True Loves. To friendship." Polly held up her glass for another toast. When she lowered the drink, she found Samuel on his knee in front of her.

"I know time hasn't been our friend, but I will cherish every moment we have together from now until eternity. Polly, will you marry me?"

Polly looked down at the old ring he held out. "Yes, of course!"

Samuel smiled and slipped the ring onto her finger and Polly sucked in a breath. Love radiated from the ring straight to her heart.

"My family only married for True Love. The stone has been in the Mannering family for generations. My mother was the last one to update it. It's a little out of style, but I wanted you to have it."

"It's perfect," Polly said before kissing him again. In the back of her mind she knew their time was limited, but tonight wasn't the night of the battle. Tonight was about love. "I love you, Samuel."

"A wedding at the Equinox!"

Polly jumped back as Grand Mistress Lauren appeared with Neferu, Agnes, and Vilma by her side.

"There's so much to do, but we can handle it all. Go, enjoy your engagement," Lauren said to them.

"Zoey knows what I want," Polly said as Jane grabbed a basket of food and drink and headed for the back door.

"I want whatever my bride does," Samuel said with eyes only for her.

Together they followed Jane to the small cottage and then *finally,* they were alone. They stood outside the heavy wooden door as Jane walked back to the main house.

"I've dreamed of this for four hundred years," Polly admitted as Samuel took her in his arms.

"So have I, love. I've had four hundred years to come up with the perfect night."

Polly laughed as Samuel swooped her up into his arms and carried her into the cottage, into his heart and into his bed.

5

Polly didn't care if she walked up the path to the standing stones in a burlap sack as long as Samuel was there to meet her. Grand Mistress Lauren planned everything while Polly and Samuel spent the night together. Tonight would serve as their honeymoon instead of taking one after the wedding. They'd learned that tomorrow was not guaranteed after what they'd witnessed in the new prophecy. While love and celebration were here now, there was war in the future.

Polly pushed it all aside. She had today. As she walked the path from the cottage to the standing stones, she took the flowers handed to her by the families who'd come to the wedding. Samuel stood next to Grand Master Magnus with Slade by his side. Grand Mistress Lauren stood on Magnus's other side with Zoey opposite Slade.

Polly looked toward her love, her future, her happiness, and smiled with pure joy. She would remember today forever. The way Samuel looked at her, the way she felt when Magnus laid a cloth embroidered with Samuel's family crest over their joined hands, and the way she felt when they were pronounced husband and wife.

The six of them hadn't told anyone about the prophecy as if by unspoken agreement. There was time for that tomorrow. Tonight, they danced among the stones, celebrating and offering up good thoughts and thanks to the Goddess. They'd let everyone have one last hurrah before they told the council the bad news.

"I love you," Samuel whispered into her ear as he held her close and swayed to the music. "I think it's time for me to show you how much." Samuel swung Polly up into his arms to a resounding cheer from their friends.

Polly laced her hands together around Samuel's neck and laughed as he ran from the stones to their little cottage. While it may not be happily ever after, it was happily for now and Polly vowed to cherish every moment with her True Love until their time was at an end.

Jane was up early making breakfast for the meeting when Zoey joined her in the kitchen. Zoey was the first witch friend Jane had since, well, forever. Her father kept her separate from other witches while she was growing up. Then he'd betrayed her by making a marriage contract with the horrible Ian—a contract that gave him her powers upon marriage. It was Zoey who had protected her and given her the strength to find and use her own powers. So Jane was glad when it was Zoey who came into the kitchen when it was still dark out to help with the breakfast. She'd known this talk was coming and it was finally time to have it.

"Can I help with anything?" Zoey asked. Jane nodded and laid out the ingredients for muffins.

"Let's bake and talk," Jane said before taking a deep breath.

"You know something and it's not good," Zoey said sadly. "Well, lay it on me. It can't be worse than your betrothal to Ian."

Jane gave a little chuckle. Leave it to Zoey to make her laugh at a time like this. It was hard being isolated at the stones, but Zoey came monthly to spend the day with her and that made it easier. Plus, now that they were open for business again, witches from all over the world were starting to trickle in to partake in the old traditions and the healing powers of the stones.

"After your last visit, I started to have dreams," Jane admitted. "I should have told you sooner, but I thought they were just dreams until I heard the prophecy."

"The stone keeper is supposed to see things. I'm actually surprised you didn't see the prophecy, or did you?" Zoey asked.

"Galen is the stronger of us in terms of the stone keepers' powers since he was born to it. He has that and the ability to heal. It was very helpful being a doctor before becoming the stone keeper. I still feel as if we're learning so much about our calling. Luckily his grandmother left lots of journals. Anyway, the dreams were about my mother. You know I saw her killed during Alexander's massacre."

Zoey nodded as she measured out her flour. "Yes. You told me that you saw your parents killed and your aunt thought you'd be safe in Ian's room, not knowing he was behind the attack too."

"My aunt, Loralei Farrington, got me to safety and then went back to see if she could get my parents out. She was very close with her brother, my father. As you all know, the Farrington line is a very old and powerful one. However, my mother's was too. She was just as strong until she married my father. I don't know if he sucked the power from her with his isolation or if she just never used it."

"A witch's form of emotional abuse," Zoey said sadly. "Some men can't handle powerful women."

"Look at me. I'm more powerful than my father ever was, at least according to Agnes and Vilma, and he sold my powers off to Ian," Jane said, the bitterness of betrayal still in her voice. "But in my dreams, it's my mother who is coming to me. She's in the stones and she's calling to me, but I can't hear her. I rush to her, but when I get there she's gone. Instead, I see the six of us, you, Slade, Polly, Samuel, myself, and Galen. We're together with our hands linked. Then my mother appears over us. She says something and I can tell it's urgent, but I can't hear her. I wake up yelling for her to speak up." Jane blew out a breath. The dream had seemed to become more urgent as the days passed. Her mother was desperately trying to tell her something, but what?

"The six of us again. Just like the vision I had," Zoey said as she absently stirred the muffin mix. "That must mean something."

"It means you should have talked to me sooner."

Jane jumped in surprise at the new voice. She turned to see Grand Mistress Lauren sitting at the kitchen table.

"You have to stop doing that," Zoey said with a roll of her eyes. "Grand mistress or not, it's creepy."

"Apparently I have to eavesdrop or I won't learn anything. My little witches are keeping secrets."

Jane felt like a kid being called out by a teacher. "I'm sorry, Grand Mistress. We wanted Polly and Samuel to have a day of celebration before this started."

"What exactly is *this*?" the grand mistress asked with her arms crossed unhappily over her chest.

"That's why we called the meeting," Zoey said, stepping in to defend Jane like she always did. She was a true friend.

"Then I'll tell everyone to hurry up." Grand Mistress Lauren closed her eyes briefly and Jane clasped her hands to her ears. It sounded like a siren was going off in her head.

"I think that'll do!" Zoey yelled, as she too clasped her hands over her ears even though the sound was entirely in their heads.

In seconds, the entire Tenebris and Claritase councils were in the stone keepers' house grumbling about the early wake-up call. Jane tried to smile to greet them, but the worry sat too heavy on her heart to do so.

As soon as everyone was in the living room, Grand Mistress Lauren called the meeting to order. "Witches have been keeping secrets. This morning we lay it all out and work together to figure out whatever these secrets mean. Jane, go first."

Jane took a deep breath and with her hand held tightly by her loving husband, told of her dream. It was time to admit their peaceful existence of the past nine months was over.

"A traitor, a love taken, families destroyed all for power. A masquerade hiding evil has been in place too long. It's time to reveal who is under the mask. Only a power stronger than True Love can defeat the dark magic as evil as this," Zoey said, repeating Helena's words to the councils.

Everyone was quiet for a moment and then everyone started talking at once.

"What power is stronger than True Love?" Raiden of the Tenebris council asked.

Another round of everyone talking at once started up again. Slade kept his hand on hers. When Zoey looked around, she saw Jane and Galen and Polly and Samuel were each in a similar embrace. This, right here, was True Love. Raiden asked a valid question, what was stronger than the love between soul mates?

Grand Mistress Lauren held up her hand to quiet everyone. "Taken together with Jane's dreams, we need to go to the stones for guidance. Maybe together we can gather enough power to see a vision.

"Wait," Galen said, stopping them. "This doesn't have to

do with you all. It has to do with Jane. It's her mother trying to reach her. It needs to be Jane who does it and Jane alone. The stones have spoken. It's to be so."

Zoey looked over at her friend who stood, ashen faced but stoic.

"I can't go with you, but I'm in your heart," Galen said to her before kissing his wife.

Zoey gave her an encouraging nod of her head as Jane looked at her. "Remember, you are stronger than you realize. You're safe in the stones. Let your power free."

Lauren and Magnus nodded in agreement and Jane turned on shaky legs. She walked slowly to the door and then she was gone.

The people inside the house broke off into small groups to discuss what had happened. Galen went to the window to watch his love on a journey he couldn't help with. Slade and Samuel joined him at the window. They'd help Jane in a heartbeat if she needed it because they were friends. Was friendship the key? Was friendship more powerful than True Love?

"We knew something was coming," her father said quietly as he wrapped his arm around her shoulder. "How are you doing, Jellybean?"

"Not too great, Dad. I've been feeling off since the vision."

"I know."

Zoey turned to her father. "You do?"

Her father nodded. "You're my daughter. Of course I know when you're not feeling well."

"Do you know what will happen?" Zoey asked the question she didn't know if she wanted answered.

"I don't know how this all ends, but I know a bit about your future. However, your future is not for me to tell. It's for you to experience. I also know we need to get back to Moonshine Hollow as soon as Jane is done. Don't you feel it? I wonder if it's what's making you feel bad?" her father questioned.

"It feels like I'm being held down. It's hard to take a full breath even though I know my lungs work. My heart pounds and my stomach feels as if I'm on a boat," Zoey admitted.

Her father nodded. "I feel most of that too, especially the weight of dread. It's coming. And once again it's up to my daughter to defeat it. I would take your place if I could. I might not be in the vision but I'll be there by your side. I'm your father and I will die to protect you."

Zoey turned into her father and threw her arms around him. "I love you, Dad."

"I love you too, Jellybean."

Jane sat cross-legged in the center of the stones. Her eyes were closed, and her hands were resting on her knees, palms up. It looked as if she was meditating but she wasn't. She was gathering all her powers and focusing them on one thing–her mother.

Jane opened her eyes at the feeling of warmth surrounding her. She was reaching out for her mother when her powers shot from her fingers and into the stones. A glow of light shot into the air above the stones and that's when Jane saw her mother.

Jane watched it play out like a movie above her. Her mother was young and happy as she stood by someone Jane had come to know as her mother's sister, Eileen. "Aurora, we are Kendricks. We're strong and powerful in our own right. You don't need to marry a Farrington because of their power. You know their reputation," Jane's Aunt Eileen said.

"But Anwir isn't like that. He loves me, Eileen," Jane's mother protested.

"We will always be here for you, Aurora. Remember your own strength." Eileen rested her forehead against her sister's and then the image faded.

A new image appeared and Jane saw her mother pregnant. Her father appeared and placed his hand on the swollen belly. His face dropped. "It's a girl. You have one purpose, Aurora, and you failed at it just like you failed at everything else. I need a boy. The Farrington line must go on."

"It will. I've seen it."

"What have you seen? Your powers aren't strong enough to have visions. They're weak like you."

Her mother shook her head. "If we love this girl, a boy of even greater power will follow."

Jane's father stopped and stared at Aurora's stomach with disgust. "For your sake, let's hope you're right."

Jane's father left the image, but the image didn't leave. Instead, her mother bowed her head, rested her hands on her belly, and began to whisper. "Unto you, my daughter, I give my powers to surround you with love and protection. Unto you, my daughter, I give my powers to surround you with love and protection . . ." she chanted over and over again. Jane watched as her mother's hands glowed with the power of magic from the Kendrick family. The glow shifted from her hands to her belly and then disappeared along with the image.

A new image formed. One of her father, mother, and her father's sister, Loralei. "It's a good match, Aurora," Loralei was saying. "Ian is young, but ambitious and powerful. Jane will make the family proud. Why don't you seek the advice of the stone keeper?"

Jane's mother nodded and reached for her sister-in-law. "Thank you, Loralei. That's very wise of you."

"Then to the stone keeper we will go," Anwir said before kissing Jane on her forehead. "Off to pack, Jane."

Aunt Loralei took her hand and gave her a wink. "Come on, I'll help you pack."

Jane and Loralei left the image, but her father and mother didn't.

"You promised me a son, yet it's been decades and you haven't conceived once. I've tried to love her, but to no avail. I'm marrying her off and that's the end of it. I might as well use her to advance our family standing."

"If you're unhappy with Jane, why don't we send her to my family? Eileen will take her in."

Jane's father grabbed her mother and shook her. "They've done nothing to help us. Your family abandoned us. Neither Jane nor yourself are to ever see those traitors again!"

The image dimmed and then a new one formed.

It was her dream. Her mother was at the stones. "Jane! I must warn you." This time there was sound to her mother's cries. Instead of disappearing again, an image of the six of them appeared with her mother. "The masquerade started long ago with each of you, but now you must work together to unmask the traitors. I gave you the power before you were born. You've had it all along. Your time to use it is now. Pull on the love that is even stronger than True Love. May the Goddess protect you and give you strength to do what I was unable to do—to stand up against evil."

The light was gone. Jane's powers were exhausted as she fell back onto the ground and everything went black.

. . .

"Jane!" Galen called to her as she felt herself being shaken awake.

"Drink this, dear." A straw was shoved into her mouth and she drank. She felt her powers flicker back to life as she opened her eyes and looked up at Vilma holding one of her magic shakes that helped replenish a witch.

Her husband looked worried as he held her. "I need to give you an exam. Are you hurt?"

Jane shook her head. "I'm fine. I just used all my powers. I'll be up and at it in seconds after I finish Vilma's drink."

"We saw your power lighting up the stones. Did you see your mother?" Zoey asked.

"I did. The six of us . . . somehow we played a role in this from the beginning. I'm not sure how, but that's why it's up to us to fight this evil. I also learned my father was an asshole and my mother gave me all her powers when she was pregnant to protect me." Jane went on to tell them everything she saw.

"I'm sorry to interrupt," Magnus said. "But we need to get back to Moonshine Hollow now. And Jane, your family needs to come too."

"I'll let them know." Galen was already pulling out his phone and sending a text to Aunt Eileen.

"I don't have enough power left to transport," Jane admitted feeling a little embarrassed.

"Not an issue," Lauren said. "Let's get back to the house, pack everything you'll need, and I'll transport you both. I feel it too, Magnus. Something is very wrong in Moonshine Hollow."

7

Sometimes the hardest thing to do is to wait. Slade stood with Zoey by his side as Jane and Galen packed. It was decided they'd all travel together. They'd face whatever waited for them in Moonshine Hollow together. Slade could feel the tension rolling off his wife. Even his normally calm father-in-law was pacing.

Slade couldn't feel what they were feeling. However, his warrior heart was ready to fight. It was hard to wait and not charge into battle. Instead, he motioned for Samuel and Polly to join him.

"Are you ready to fight?" Slade asked his fiercest warriors.

Samuel nodded, but then reached for Polly. Slade knew the feeling. Fighting for your True Love gave you added power, but also added worry. It was hard to go into battle when half of you was watching out for your wife. Especially when your wife was likely the key to the outcome of the battle.

"I'm ready too," Polly said, and Slade could see that. She

was practically glowing with power. He looked at his wife who was similarly shimmering.

Slade's eyes met Samuel's and his friend shrugged. He didn't know what was causing it either.

Agnes and Vilma noticed as well and walked over to join them. Agnes and Vilma had taken Slade under their motherly wings once they realized he was Zoey's True Love. The two of them easily filled the parental role not only for him, but also for every witch in Moonshine Hollow.

"You two are shimmering," Agnes said bluntly.

Zoey looked over to Polly and then down at herself. "Huh, that's interesting."

"I'm ready to fight," Polly said. "I feel a surge of energy to protect the town."

"Me too," Zoey added.

"I do too, but I'm not shimmering," Slade said.

"Hmm," Vilma grunted. "I'll think on it. What do you think about how you're linked?"

Slade shook his head. "I have no idea. Samuel and I go back to fighting against Alexander."

"I wasn't even born when Alexander turned traitor," Zoey pointed out.

"I'm ready," Jane called out, joining them with her husband.

"You're shimmering too," Slade said to her. It wasn't as noticeable as Polly or Zoey because her powers still weren't back to normal levels, but Jane had an undeniable shimmer of her own.

"Huh," Vilma grunted again and looked over to Agnes who was similarly staring at the three ladies.

"Your men aren't shimmering though," Agnes said absently as if thinking it over.

"Men don't shimmer," Slade said as she crossed his arms over his chest. "We sweat."

Zoey snickered beside him as Magnus and Lauren joined them. They looked between the three women and their brows furrowed in thought.

"We know. We're looking into it," Vilma answered their unspoken question.

"Okay then. Let's be ready for anything," Lauren said to them. Together the council formed a circle. "On three. One. Two. Three." *Poof.*

"Zoey! Slade!" Slade heard an old lady yell from the front door of their house. The entire council was in their living room. Slade dropped Zoey's hand and raced for the door.

"Peach? What's going on?" he asked the sweet old woman who had a mischievous streak when it came to fights with her husband, Otis. They were the town's entertainment for the pranks they played on each other.

"We've been trying to call you. No one is answering at the sheriff's department. Oh, it's horrible!" Tears streaked the wrinkled face of the woman who always brought fresh baked goods to the sheriff's office *just because.*

"I'm sorry, ma'am," Samuel said, joining Slade at the door. "Polly and I got married."

Peach's eyes lit up briefly. "About time!" Then she shook her head. "The cemetery. You have to get to the cemetery."

Slade wanted to just *poof* there, but not with Peach following. Instead, the council crammed into cars and took off to the other end of town where the church and cemetery were.

Cars filled the parking lot and street. They didn't even

bother finding spots. Slade had to park a block away and they ran between cars, around the church, and were stopped by a wall of citizens, both human and witch.

"Thank Goddess you're here," Fern said. She was the Claritase's family history expert. "When we couldn't find the council, we figured you all were away on business. We tried to fix it, but we couldn't." Fern nodded to some of the other witches, both Claritase and Tenebris, and then shook her head. "It's very traumatic for the town."

Slade could tell. There was the sound of crying all around them. "What is it?"

"See for yourself," Fern said sadly. "The sheriff is here!" She was loud enough to get the people to part so Slade and the council could walk through.

"It's horrible," Fay whimpered. Fay was another member of the Irises, the older married women's club.

"I've never seen something so disrespectful," Bart, the bartender at the Opossum Lodge, said as he ran his hand over his long beard.

"Who would do something like this?" Maribelle said with tears in her eyes as she clung to her husband, Dale.

Slade finally made it through and stopped dead in his tracks. Every coffin in the cemetery was above ground and open. Loved ones from the funeral last week all the way back to Earnest, the founder of Moonshine Hollow, were exposed.

"We tried to fix it," Fern said, keeping her voice low to let him know they'd tried magic on it. "We couldn't. It's black magic."

Zoey suddenly gasped next to him. When he turned to look at her, she was grabbing her throat as if she were choking.

"Zoey!" he yelled as she collapsed. She clawed at her throat as he dropped to his knees in front of her.

"She's choking," Peach cried.

"I got it," Galen shoved his way forward and they all ignored the surprise at seeing their former town doctor who should be in Scotland. Galen put his hands on Zoey and then froze. "Get her to the clinic. Now."

Slade was already moving. He had Zoey in his arms and was running. The council formed a wall to stop people from following and the second they had him blocked he transported them to a room in the clinic. A second later Galen was there with Lauren.

"It's black magic," Galen said. "It's killing her."

A moment later Magnus and Jane ran into the room. "I feel it. It's like tar is filling her throat," Magnus said.

"Help me," Lauren said as she rubbed her hands together pulling all her magic forward.

"Why isn't it working?" Slade asked as he watched helplessly as his wife struggled to breath.

Suddenly Galen stiffened. "Are you okay?" Slade asked as Galen's eyes opened wide. He lifted his hands up and white light shot from the palms like a spotlight. It wasn't the same as Zoey's. His was more blinding.

"Oh my Goddess," Jane gasped. "What's happening?"

"Get back," Galen ordered. "I don't know what's happening, but I know what I have to do." Everyone stepped back from Zoey even as her lips turned blue. Galen stepped forward and aimed his palms at Zoey's neck. Her eyes shot open and her body began to shake as Galen began chanting in a language Slade had never heard.

"It's the old language," Lauren whispered in disbelief. "The language of the Goddess. No one speaks it anymore and most don't even remember it. I didn't know Galen knew it."

"He doesn't," Jane whispered back.

The light from his hands grew brighter and Zoey's body bowed on the exam table. She let out a cry that had Slade running toward her. Only Magnus stopped him. He wrapped his arms around Slade and held on. "Hold on, son. Let him work. Look, she's not blue anymore."

Slade couldn't see that. All he could see was that his love was in pain. Then the light grew so bright he had to close his eyes. Just as fast as the blinding light had appeared, it was gone.

Slade opened his eyes to find Galen sitting on the floor and Zoey taking deep breaths.

"What in the name of the Goddess was that?" Zoey gasped out between big breaths.

"I don't know," Galen said, shaking his head as Magnus helped him up. "As soon as I felt whatever was hurting Zoey, it was like something took over my body and knew what to do. I almost did that light thing at the cemetery."

The door opened and everyone went quiet. Doris Bleacher, the most rigid and forbidding receptionist you've ever met, glared at them. Her face was pinched and her style was still stuck in the 1960s. "What are you doing here? How did you get by me?"

"Zoey choked on some food and we came in through the back door," Lauren answered with an air of authority. What Doris hasn't realized was that the clinic was now run entirely by witches. They'd tried to get Doris to retire, but she simply refused and everyone was too afraid of her to push the matter further.

"Well, don't think you can get away without paying for the office visit. We accept credit cards now." With a huff of annoyance, she shut the door and went out into the lobby behind the fortress of her Formica and metal desk.

Zoey reached for him and Slade was there. "How do you feel, sweetness?"

"Much better. But, Slade, we need access to the cemetery and we need the citizens of Moonshine Hollow far away."

"I'll have Samuel get to work on that."

"Help him. The sooner we get it done, the better. It feels like an infection of the town has taken root. We need to take care of it. Get me some of Vilma and Agnes's drink and let's get to work."

"Sweetness, you almost died. You need to rest." Slade saw Zoey's eyes narrow in response. Yeah, that wasn't going to happen.

"Jellybean, Slade is correct. This stuff went after you, and you alone. We need to find out why," her father said before receiving the same narrow-eyed look.

"We'll take Galen with us," Zoey said, sitting up and swinging her legs over the edge of the table.

"I'll call in reinforcements," Lauren said. "Magnus, call the Tenebris."

It was settled. Slade didn't like it, but he knew Zoey well enough to know she wasn't going to back down. "I'll get the area roped off. Do not join me until we're set up. Can you at least do that for me?"

His wife smiled at him. "Yes. I'll drink my drink and maybe we can have Fern and Neferu look into it why it's affecting only me. Between the family trees and the historian, maybe we can find a clue."

"Good idea. I'll do that right now," Lauren said.

"I'll have Raiden and Niles look into it as well," Magnus said. "Maybe we can find something in the Tenebris records. After all, we know Alexander used some dark magic. This has to be one of his followers since Ian was involved as well."

"We have a lot to do. We'll meet tonight at the cemetery," Lauren ordered. When Zoey began to argue, Lauren shook her head just once. "End of discussion. We have a lot to do in a very short time. Now, let's get to work."

8

Nothing felt right to Zoey. She felt off. She'd been feeling off for days, but today pushed her over the edge. Even after what Galen had done, she felt a presence inside her. Good or evil, she didn't know, but she knew it was real.

Slade and Samuel had promised everyone they'd bring in morticians to respectfully reinter all of their loved ones tonight. Magically, eight-foot portable walls were found in the sheriff's department storage area and erected around the cemetery after Slade had quartered off most of lower Main Street.

Galen, Jane, and Zoey spent the day in her living room being cared for by Agnes and Vilma and were now feeling the full flow of their magic. Something had changed in Galen though. He stood taller and seemed surer of himself even though he was unsure about everything else.

"Jane!" The front door opened and Jane's Aunt Eileen and the rest of the Kendrick clan rushed into the living room. "Are you okay? We've heard about what's happening. I'm so sorry it took so long to get here. I had to travel to more than a few countries to find all the old family records."

"We need Fern and Neferu to see these," Zoey said.

"You rang?" Fern giggled as she walked through with Neferu, who looked annoyed at anyone under a millennium in age, just on general principles. Niles and Raiden followed with boxes in their arms.

"I brought the Kendrick records," Eileen said as she pointed to the boxes on the table. She sat next to Jane and held her. "Something's different about you. You're shimmering. And why does Galen look different?"

"That I can answer," Neferu said. "Not the shimmering, but about Galen. Niles, the book please."

Niles seemed like a young pup to Neferu, but the young man was as sharp as a whip. "It's right here." He pulled an ancient tome from one of the boxes and handed it to Neferu.

"These are the original notes from Grand Mistress Celesta, our first Grand Mistress and appointed by the Goddess herself. I'll read from them. *Today I had a vision from the Goddess. It took me to these large stones that appeared to be standing. Under a night sky filled with green waves, the Goddess spoke to me. A man and a woman appeared in the distance. They were to be Keepers of the Stones. They were the healers and protectors of witches, just as we heal and protect humans. In the stones we can find nourishment for our powers and in the stone keepers we find healers for our powers. The Goddess told me that she conveyed unto the keepers powers of their own. For where there is darkness there must be light. Where there is evil, there must be goodness. The stone keepers have the ability to keep those powers in balance so that evil may never snuff out goodness, so that Earth and humans will never be overtaken by darkness. That is the stone keepers' true role.*" Neferu closed the book and looked at Galen.

"I keep the balance of power shifted toward goodness."

Galen nodded as if he accepted and understood it completely.

"That's right. And what you were chanting in the old language to heal Zoey translates to *I call on the power of the Goddess and light to banish the dark,*" Niles told him.

"Okay, so now that makes sense why Galen is in the visions," Jane said.

"What visions?" Aunt Eileen asked.

Jane filled her family in as quickly as she could. Zoey could see the anger as Jane completed the story and called for the council to come immediately.

"Why did he call you traitors?" Jane asked.

"We tried to help your mother escape your father. We hid her and you from him when you were five years old. We saw your full potential but luckily, your father didn't. We knew we had to get you away from him or he'd kill you for it. We got you both away from him and taught you to hide your power. Then we erased your memory of it, locking the strongest of your powers away to protect you. When your father found out your mother was missing, he tore the world apart looking for her. I don't know why. He hated her. However, because we tried to help you escape, we were labeled traitors."

"He wanted to keep power over us," Jane said sadly.

"Actually," Raiden said, stepping in, "I can help here."

"He wanted the Kendrick power. Your mother was technically the strongest Claritase at that time. Your father was the strongest Farrington at the time."

Eileen nodded. "That's why we hid your power. Your father wanted a son. A son to take over the Tenebris and Claritase. He knew with the combined power of the two families they'd be able to. What he hadn't counted on was your mother giving all her powers to you. He kept trying to take Aurora's powers, but she had only the smallest amount left and it frustrated him to no end. When you showed your first spark of power, we had to protect you. Then after Anwir found you and your mother, he made sure we'd never find you again. We didn't see you again until the night Alexander attacked. Luckily I'd left my children at home. The fight started and I fought to get to you."

Jane frowned. "But it was too late. My parents were killed and Aunt Loralei got me to safety, or so she thought."

"Thank Goddess you were saved. However, you parents weren't killed quite the way you might think," Eileen said softly. "Your father killed Aurora when he took the last of her powers to fight for Alexander. The last I saw of Anwir, he was battling Polly's mother. She was a fierce warrior." Eileen dipped her head in Polly's direction in honor of her mother.

"My parents didn't survive that night," Polly said softly from where the rest of the council had *poofed* in and were then gathered.

"Most parents didn't," Eileen said sadly. "As soon as whatever was keeping us from transporting disappeared, whoever was still left alive got away and we began the centuries of hiding.

"Have you found anything that links the six of them?" Lauren asked the researchers.

"Not yet, but we will. If it's to be found, it'll be in these boxes," Neferu said with surety.

"Then you all stay here and look through them while we head back to the cemetery," Magnus ordered.

Zoey felt Slade's hand cover hers. He didn't need to say anything. She saw how concerned he was for her. She felt it in his touch and through their True Love connection. This was not about her though. This was about her town and her friends.

"Come on. Let's check out the cemetery and get it put back to rights." Zoey stood, trying to pretend seeing all the remains didn't bother her. It did. Maribelle was a wreck after seeing her family members like that. If for no other reason than to bring her best friend peace and comfort, Zoey would do everything she could to put it to rights.

"What do you think?" Zoey's father asked her as they stood in the middle of the cemetery.

"I'm practically choking on the evil again. I can smell it. I can taste it. I can feel it trying to take over my powers. It's sticking to me like glue and looking for a way inside." Zoey was beyond freaked out. "Does anyone else feel it?"

All the witches nodded. Some gave a little shiver like something walked over their graves.

"Keep together," Grand Mistress Lauren said, motioning for them to gather closely. "Link hands. We're stronger together than separate. If you think the black magic will overtake you, leave and see Galen to be cleansed."

Zoey held Slade's hand with her right and Polly's hand with her left. Samuel was on Polly's other side, and Jane was on Slade's far side. "Wait!" Zoey called out as the large circle of witches were spreading out with their hands clasped together. "We need Galen in the circle."

"Why?" Jane asked as she leaned forward to see around Slade.

"I don't know how, but I just know." Zoey didn't know how to explain it. She just felt it within her soul that the six of them had to do this together.

"Galen, come stand with me. If Zoey says you need to be

here, you need to be here," Jane said, holding out her hand for her husband.

"Alternate Tenebris and Claritase," Zoey said suddenly as if she had no ability to stop herself. It just came out. "Together. Linked together we are stronger."

No one questioned her. Polly and Samuel switched places and over the next couple of minutes witches from all over the world were linked together.

"Are we good?" her father asked her.

Zoey nodded. "We're good now. Galen needs to chant what he did when he was saving me."

"How do you know that?" Galen asked.

Zoey wished she knew. It was just coming out of her mouth. "How did you know what to do when you were saving me?"

"Understood," Galen said, taking a deep breath. He began to chant in the old language. The bond between him and Jane grew stronger. Soon, Galen was aglow with that powerful white light. He shone like a lighthouse sweeping the light over the inner circle.

"Everyone chant," Zoey called out and the hundreds of witches began to chant along with Galen. The light traveled from linked hand to linked hand until it formed a ring of light around the cemetery.

Zoey felt the black magic fighting back. She felt it climbing from the shadows and reaching for them. She felt Slade's hand tighten on hers as the black magic seemed to take form. Shadows pooled together. Darkness crept forward to escape the light from the witches until it materialized in the center of the circle. A dark form took shape from out of the black magic.

"Keep going! Close in on it!" Zoey yelled as the witches were now each clutching the hands they held. Zoey took a step forward and then together the circle of chanting witches closed in on the thick tar-like shadow form.

A shriek was let out when the first ray of light hit the form. The sound wasn't human. It was more animal than anything. The sound intensified as the light focused on it. The form twisted and bent as it screeched louder and louder. Pain shot through Zoey's head as the form writhed in the light.

I'm coming for you.

Zoey heard the voice in her mind and knew it was coming from whoever was wielding the black magic. "You won't win! We beat you tonight and we'll beat you every time you come after us," Zoey shouted, drawing strange looks from the people who had heard her.

This was just a warm-up.

"Why are you doing this?" Zoey shouted at the rapidly shrinking form.

Revenge. Wait until you see what I do next.

The voice laughed and then there was silence. The form in the circle of light vanished and the weight of evil pressing down on Zoey disappeared.

"The black magic is gone," Lauren said with relief. "Great work."

With a flick of Laruen's hand, the coffins were all closed.

"Everyone take a casket and get them re-buried," Lauren ordered as she walked toward Zoey. "What happened just now?"

Polly, Samuel, Slade, Jane, Galen, and her father formed a tight circle around Zoey and Lauren so no one could overhear. "I heard a voice in my head. It was the person wielding the black magic."

"Who was it?" Slade asked.

Zoey shook her head. "I don't know. I couldn't even tell if it was male or female."

"What did it say?" her father asked.

Zoey repeated the conversation and everyone looked worriedly at each other.

"Revenge? Against us? Why?" Polly wondered.

"This has to do with Ian. We all heard the scream when he was killed. Are they coming after us for that?" Magnus asked.

"Maybe," Zoey said. "But remember I passed out from the black magic down by the creek last year. Black magic has been here before. Revenge for taking him, maybe. But they were planning something before then. Something that involved Jane and her powers."

"You need to get Aunt Eileen to undo whatever it was she did when you were five," Polly said as she looked at Jane. "Maybe by releasing those memories, it will uncover a clue. Also, if you're as powerful as they say, you can use your powers against whoever is behind this."

"Great idea," Lauren said with a nod of her head.

Zoey saw Jane nibble on her bottom lip. She did that when she was nervous. "I don't know if I want to remember everything about my childhood, but I'll do it."

"Now, what can we do to protect ourselves for the next wave of black magic?" Slade asked the question Zoey dreaded.

"I don't know," she admitted. And she didn't. It killed her not to know how to protect her town and her friends. "Galen, do you have any ideas?"

Galen shook his head. "I'm sorry. I don't know what to make of any of this. When I'm needed my powers seem to know what to do and just do it."

"Let's finish cleaning up the cemetery and then rest

tonight. Tomorrow the councils will gather and help Eileen with anything she needs to free Jane's powers. Hopefully Neferu, Fern, Niles, and Raiden will have found some more information for us by then. Then we can work on putting the pieces back together," Magnus told them.

They all agreed to meet at Zoey's house at nine the next morning. Zoey turned back to help put the cemetery back to rights but her mind wandered. *Who* was behind this and what were they going to do next?

9

Jane paced across Zoey's bakery kitchen early the next morning. She hadn't slept a wink. She gave up on sleep at five in the morning and knew Zoey would be up. She's scared Zoey half to death when she *poofed* into the bakery.

"I don't know about having everyone there," Jane said as she wrung her fingers together. "I don't like the idea of everyone just staring at me."

Zoey had been listening to her patiently for the past twenty minutes.

"So, why don't you tell us who you want there and I'll do everything I can to make that happen," Zoey said calmly as she poured flour into a large industrial mixer. Even though Zoey could use her magic to make her treats, she always preferred to do it by hand. It was one of the things Jane really liked about her.

"I don't think they'd let me," Jane said with a sigh as she stopped to take a seat on a stool. Chance, Zoey's black Labrador, sat in front of her and rested his large square head on her knee.

"You won't know until you ask. What would make you feel more comfortable?" Zoey asked.

"The six of us. Every day I feel more connected to our little group."

"Okay, do you think you can be comfortable with Lauren and my father there too?"

Jane took a deep breath and then let it out on a sigh. "Your dad has become like a father to me. He's really taken me in. Grand Mistress Lauren still makes me nervous."

"Nervous? I make you nervous?"

"Grand Mistress! You have *got* to stop doing that," Zoey yelled as the leader of the Claritase just popped into the kitchen. "This is why you make people nervous."

Jane saw Lauren's teal eyes dim as her lips curved downward into a frown. "I'm so sorry. I just want to keep an eye on my witches. You're all like my own little witchlings."

"Don't say it," Zoey groaned. "I know why you are here. Don't you dare ask me."

"Ask what?" Lauren blinked her eyes innocently.

"I'm not pregnant, okay?"

"I didn't ask anything," Lauren said with a sly smile.

Jane laughed and then looked at Zoey apologetically. If Zoey spoke that freely with the grand mistress, Jane could too. Lauren was just another witch after all. "Grand Mistress," Jane said before her nerve failed her, "I have a request."

"Yes, Jane?" Lauren asked as she plucked a hot muffin from the tray and popped a piece into her mouth.

"I'm nervous about this morning. I don't know what to expect and I don't want to be embarrassed. I would like to request only the six of us be there. The six from the prophecy."

Jane waited while the grand mistress ate another bite of

the muffin. Her heart beat loudly and her palms were sweaty as she wondered if she were going to get into trouble. It made sense to her now, why she avoided conflict. She'd grown up watching her father berate her mother.

"If you allow Magnus and me to sit quietly in the back of the room, I'll allow it," Grand Mistress Lauren finally said. "And, I'm sorry if I make you nervous. I don't mean to."

"Thank you," Jane said with a little smile.

"So, since I can't ask Zoey anymore, any chance for a little witchling?" Lauren asked Jane, looking as excited as Chance did when Jane gave him a bone.

Jane laughed and shook her head as Zoey gave a fist pump in the air. "Yes! Ask other people. Don't pin all your hopes on me," Zoey said with enthusiasm. "Sorry, Jane. Meet the bus I'm throwing you under. It's named Lauren."

Jane laughed, but her heart wasn't in it. "We've been trying, but so far nothing. Also, will we have witchlings? I'm not sure how this will work with him being stone keeper."

"I'm sure all will be well," Lauren said as she placed her hand on Jane's. "Poor thing. You have far too much on your mind right now to worry about witchlings."

"Why have you never said that to me?" Zoey asked as she tossed a kitchen towel at the back of Lauren's head.

"Because she thinks if you get pregnant, everyone else will," Agnes said from beside Jane.

Jane jumped in surprise as Agnes and Vilma reached for a muffin and Zoey groaned again. "That's four people this morning. Am I going to have to spell-proof my kitchen to prevent y'all from *poofing* in here? I mean, the door is right there. Just knock!"

Agnes snorted, Vilma rolled her eyes, Lauren looked confused, and Jane smothered a laugh.

"We thought we'd help with the breakfast rush. We

knew it was going to be a doozy today with all the talk of the cemetery," Agnes said as she waved a hand, and a mop went off on its own to clean the floors out front.

Vilma waved her hand and fresh flowers appeared on the tables and the coffee pot turned on. "See. We're here to help."

"Thank you," Zoey said with a kind smile for the ladies who looked after all the younger members of the Claritase as if they were their favorite aunts or grandmothers. "Wait, what do you mean you think no one will get pregnant until I do?"

Jane thought Agnes was teasing when she'd said that, but Zoey clearly didn't think she was joking.

"Well," Lauren said, looking a little embarrassed. That one look made Jane relax. Lauren really was just another witch. There was no reason to be nervous around her. "No one married until you. Now we've had over thirty marriages across the world and not a single witchling? It's too strange. People have waited four hundred years to get married. I can guarantee they aren't going to wait one more day to try to have a baby."

"This has nothing to do with me. I'm not preventing them from making babies," Zoey said.

"I think you have to be the first. It's your fate to one day lead the Claritase. You had to be the first to challenge Alexander. You had to be the first to marry. I think you have to be the first to have a baby. A baby your father tells me is very important to our future."

"No, no, no," Zoey said, shaking her head. "I'm already the key to these battles. I'm not bringing in an innocent life to stick them in that position."

"Fate has a way of deciding things on her own." Lauren's statement seemed more like a threat, but Jane knew more than anyone there that fate had a way of stepping in when needed, and least expected. Even if the person didn't know they needed a helping hand. After all, that's how Zoey met Slade, moved to Moonshine Hollow, and how Jane had found her. Fate brought them all together and fate wasn't done with them yet.

Galen sat in Slade's kitchen and looked at his watch. Jane would be there soon. He looked over his shoulder into the dining room. Neferu, Niles, Fern, and Raiden were neck-deep in paperwork, journals, and old records.

"Do you think they'll find what connects us?" Galen asked Slade.

Slade crossed his arms over his chest and glanced into the dining room. "I don't know. But I have a few ideas already."

"You do?"

Slade nodded, but didn't elaborate. He wasn't the chatty type and he wouldn't share unless he was ready.

"Slade, do you think I can protect Jane from whatever is about to happen?"

Slade uncrossed his arms and looked over Galen. "I don't know, but I think the Goddess has something up her sleeve. You have powers. We just don't know what they are. If the prophecy is right and it's up to the six of us to defeat whatever this black magic is, then yes, I think you can."

Galen was about to say more when Slade's phone rang. Slade answered and Galen was about to turn away when Slade went rigid. "Where?" he asked. "We'll be right there."

Slade hung up and Galen could tell by the way his jaw was clenched it wasn't good. "We need to get to the distillery right now," Slade told the room. "Transport to it. We don't have a second to lose."

Galen was about to get his car when Slade reached out and touched him. Suddenly Galen was at the distillery. Fire licked at him. The heat was oppressive. Samuel was yelling to evacuate the area.

Galen looked up at the distillery that provided most of the jobs to Moonshine Hollow. It was covered in a dark sticky substance and engulfed in flames.

"Niles, help Galen get the people out of here and treat the injured," Slade ordered. "Fern, set up a perimeter to prevent the fire from spreading. Neferu, control the wind so no embers float off and start a forest fire. Raiden, clear the building. Samuel, as soon as the building is clear, soak it!"

Galen gasped as Raiden walked through the fire and into the building.

"His power comes from fire," Niles said as he flicked his wrist and suddenly Galen couldn't see the distillery through the thick smoke. Smoke he somehow wasn't able to smell. "Come on, doc. We've got work to do."

"You're a doctor?" Galen asked as they began to yell for the people to move away from the distillery.

"I was many centuries ago. I try to stay up to date. Let's get going."

"Galen!" Jane yelled as she ran toward him, Zoey, Polly, Lauren, and Magnus by her side. "What's going on?"

"Fire at the distillery!" Galen yelled back. "Help us evacuate the area."

Zoey nodded and began to help along with Jane, but Polly and Magnus ran straight for the fire along with a handful of other witches that had appeared behind them.

. . .

Slade was unusual. He knew that. He was one of the few witches that had dual powers. He'd inherited both his father's fire power and his mother's water power. He wasn't alone in this, several other witches had dual powers, but it wasn't common. Today though, it worked in his favor as he cloaked himself in his powers and raced into the distillery.

"Slade! There's three more back there," Raiden said as he carried a human over each shoulder.

Slade held up his hand and called out to the water power in him. The blue light hit the fire and sizzled it out as Slade ran to the back. Two men and a woman were unconscious. Slade lifted the woman over one shoulder, but then the building creaked. It wasn't going to last long, especially if it reached the fermenting area for the moonshine.

Slade gathered the people and then transported them outside. Fern was using her earth magic to build mountains of dirt around the property and to bend the trees away from the fire. "Get Raiden to carry them down to Galen," Slade ordered.

He turned to find Neferu and Samuel glowing light blue as they controlled the fire. Polly and Magnus joined them asking what they could do.

"I need all fire witches inside to make sure no people are left inside. I need all water witches around the building, inside and out! I need all air witches to whip up some thunder clouds, and I need earth witches ready to smother any fire that escapes." Slade yelled.

Witches went running. Slade pulled the water power from deep inside the earth, from the clouds, and even the river not that far away. He could feel the area humming with magic as the witches pulled from the elements to grow their powers.

"Now!" Slade bellowed. He released the water energy from his hands into the air. Dark blue and light blue powers mixed in the air above the distillery. A loud clap of thunder erupted and rain poured down from above and even from below where the water in the earth was brought rushing up to the surface. It was working, but not as fast as he needed. Until Magnus stopped next to him.

"Help me," Magnus ordered. "Take my hand. We're going to bring the river here."

Slade immediately grabbed his father-in-law's hand. "Picture the water," Magnus ordered and Slade pictured the rushing water from the river covering the flames of the distillery.

"Now!" Magnus ordered.

Slade let his power go. Magnus had a blue power, the shade of which no one had ever seen before. Together they called to the river behind the distillery. A wall of water formed as high as the distillery.

"Everyone out!" Slade yelled as he felt his power wavering. An entire river was hard to control.

"It's clear!" Polly yelled as she appeared by his side.

"Let it go, son," Magnus said.

With a flick of their hands they directed the wall of water at the distillery. It crashed down over it, breaking the windows and flooding the inside and out. The water witches and the earth witches worked to control the water from escaping the area. After a tense and hectic time of working together, all the witches dropped their hands. The fire was out.

10

Jane and Zoey stood side by side as people cried. Galen, Lauren, Niles, and all the healing witches had worked hard to save everyone, but some distillery workers were badly injured. Witches who weren't helping control the fire were helping to dull the pain of the injured people as the witch medics worked their magic.

They set bones, they treated burns, and worked to reunite families. The entire town of Moonshine Hollow had shown up, fearful for their loved ones and the town's economy.

A thick layer of smoke had prevented anyone from seeing much. Finally the smoke began to dissipate. When it did soot-covered witches stepped from the fading smoke.

"The fire is out and we got everyone out of the building," Slade said to the large group of citizens eager for news.

"Can I go in and assess the damage?" Mr. Earnest asked. He was the owner of the distillery along with most of the town who had bought shares along the way.

"I'm sorry, it's not safe to do so right now," Slade told him.

Zoey could see the worry rolling off him for his employees and for the business that had been in his family for generations.

"Mr. Earnest," Polly said as she joined them. "I did save this for you."

Polly held up a fireproof box in one hand a giant trash bag in the other. "The original recipes," Mr. Earnest said with relief as he took the box and clung to it. "What's in the bag?"

"I scooped out as much of the starter as I could," Polly said, handing it over to Mr. Earnest who began to cry.

"Thank you so much! It's the same strand our family's used since the very beginning. We wouldn't be the same without it. Now to get it safe."

Distillery workers rushed forward. The recipe and starter were just as important to them as to Mr. Earnest.

Jane watched as they worked together to save the legacy of Moonshine Hollow. Off in the distance she would have sworn she heard laughter. Jane looked at Zoey and saw her eyes narrowing as she looked off in the distance.

"Did you hear that?" Jane asked.

"I heard laughter," Lauren said, joining them.

"Me too," Zoey said.

"Did you all just hear laughter?" Slade asked.

That laughter might have been meant to taunt, but it hit Jane hard. Gone were her nerves. Instead, anger replaced it. Someone was trying to destroy the town that took her in. The town that had protected her from Ian. The town that had given her love and a place to call home.

"We need to get my powers back now," Jane said, turning to them. "I know you're all exhausted, but I have a feeling I'm going to need them soon."

. . .

Zoey agreed. That laughter had been menacing. The witch behind the black magic was toying with them. Unfortunately, these little events were becoming increasingly dangerous for the town and people Zoey loved.

"Moonshiners!" Slade yelled so loudly it seemed to reverberate off the mountains and echo through town. The people went quiet as they turned to look at Slade. "Please, go to your homes. Samuel, Dale, and I are going to do a population check. We're going to make sure everyone is accounted for and safe. If you require medical attention, please raise your hand and we'll send you home with one of the EMTs here to treat you or we'll get you to the nearest hospital for treatment."

"Can you believe this? This is just horrible," Maribelle said as she joined Zoey, Lauren, and Jane with Clara at her side. "Dale is going to help Slade get a count to make sure no one is missing. This is just too much. First the cemetery, then this? It's like we are cursed."

Maribelle had no idea how close to the truth she was. Zoey looked over to Maribelle's husband, Dale, as he wrote down who needed to be transported to the hospital. They were a good and loving couple to each other and to the rest of the town.

"I can't believe it. I could smell the smoke all the way at my shop. I sure hope everyone is okay. What will our town do now?" Clara asked.

"We'll rebuild. We have to. The distillery is the primary source of income for most of the residents here," Maribelle told Clara. "I just wonder how it started."

"Moonshine is very combustible. It's a good thing it didn't explode," Clara told them.

"Come on, you two. We'll walk you home," Zoey said as she laced her arm through Maribelle's.

"That's okay. I see Fay over there and I want to make sure she gets home okay. She's my neighbor and the poor dear doesn't see as well as she used to. Just don't tell her that, though. I learned that the hard way," Clara said with a little laugh.

The group waved goodbye to Clara and started to follow the crowd down Stillhouse Lane toward town. People peeled off onto Runner Road and Double Run to their houses.

"Here I am," Maribelle said as she stopped at the cute cottage style house that she and Dale called home. "Thanks for walking me home. I have to admit this has shaken me up."

Zoey hugged her best friend. "I'll see you in the morning, okay?"

Maribelle nodded. "Bye Zoey."

It took a while for the council to reassemble at Zoey and Slade's house. Jane wanted to have Aunt Eileen work her magic right away, but even she knew they needed to wait for the six to arrive. They listened to Neferu, Niles, Fern, and Raiden as they worked on uncovering the past while they waited for the rest of the six.

"This is impossible," Fern said with a sigh. "Zoey, Magnus, and Galen weren't even born four hundred years ago. They can't have a connection to Slade, Polly, and Jane."

Raiden sat back and ran his hand over his head in frustration. "Polly spent most of her life in America. Jane spent most of hers in Western Europe. Samuel spent most of his in Eastern Europe."

"Well, we're True Loves. That's a connection, right?" Polly asked. "Maybe we need to be more general."

"Could it be as general as Polly's mother battled Jane's

father the night Alexander attacked the court?" Jane's aunt asked. "It's not much, but it's a thread."

Neferu nodded. "And every thread needs to be pulled. Good idea, Eileen. Let's start broadening the search to look for any similarities or any time they were in the same place at the same time."

"Alexander ordered Slade to kill my father when he was a witchling," Zoey said, and Jane gasped.

"He did? That's horrible."

"But it's another thread. Good," Neferu said as she wrote it down.

The door opened and a very tired and soot-covered Slade and Samuel walked in.

"Is anyone missing?" Zoey asked.

Slade shook his head as he came over and put his arm around Zoey. He kissed the top of her head before he answered. "No. Thank Goddess."

"I'm very glad, but we need to fix me," Jane said, drawing all the tired eyes in the room back to her. Jane was filled with an urgency she couldn't explain.

"Okay, dear. Lie down on the couch and we'll start. It's been a long time since I've done magic like this," Aunt Eileen warned.

Jane took her place on the couch as Neferu and her team vanished for the night. All that was left were the six friends, Aunt Eileen, and the two grand masters.

"Close your eyes. I want you to go back to the first memory you have," her aunt told her.

Jane closed her eyes and felt her aunt's hands cup her head. Her fingers pressed gently into Jane's temples as she thought back through her life. Her brain felt fuzzy and full as her aunt's powers filled the room.

"Go back further, Jane," her aunt said softly.

Jane remembered turning a century. She remembered turning fifty. The memories were hazier now. She felt as if she were walking through a fog in her mind in an effort to find a needle in a haystack.

Jane didn't know how long she lay there, trying to find her way in the foggy maze of her memories. However, she knew she hadn't found her earliest memory yet. She was back to being twenty years old. She remembered the fashion. The time she spent traveling with her family. The way her father would show her love and then lash out in anger. She tried to go back further, but the fog became too heavy. She pushed and pushed, but she seemed to be wandering in circles. The same memories kept coming up.

"Tell me about the memory that you keep coming back to," her aunt's voice said from far away.

"We're at the stone keeper's cottage. Mother and I weren't allowed to meet with her. Father kept us up in the stones. We opened our powers up to the Goddess. My eyes were closed for most of it, praying that I wouldn't be bound to Ian. When we heard my father leave the cottage, I opened my eyes. I was filled with dread and my mother hugged me. Her hug warmed my heart and soul as she whispered in my ear that everything would be okay," Jane told them. She could still feel the whisper of air coming from her mother's lips against her ear as she told Jane how much she was loved.

"No wonder you're having trouble remembering your past. Aurora put her own layer of protection on you," Eileen said with a sigh as she dropped her hands from Jane's head. "We need to figure out the maze your mother left before you can unlock your powers. I've done what I can. It's up to you, your memory, and your mother now."

Jane sat up and frowned. "But my mother didn't have any power left. How could she block my memory?"

"Never underestimate the power of a mother's love," Eileen told her. "I'd find a way to save my children even if it meant my death. Your mother probably hid a power reserve from your father. Not enough to do hard magic with, but enough to protect you."

Jane sighed and leaned into Galen as he slipped his arm around her. He kissed her forehead and snuggled her against his side. "Don't worry, Jane. We'll solve this puzzle together."

Jane nodded, but she didn't feel nearly as optimistic as Galen that they'd solve this. It had been over four hundred years. How was she to unlock all of her powers now? Did she even still have them?

"Why don't we go home to Scotland tonight and I'll see if Nan kept any notes that could help. As the stone keeper, she kept thousands of journals. Maybe there's an answer in one of them," Galen suggested. "We'll be back bright and early so you can sneak into the bakery and scare Zoey while you snack on her muffins."

Jane smiled weakly and tried not to cry with frustration. She knew Galen would be up all night scouring the pages of his grandmother's books. If there were something to find, he'd find it.

11

Slade looked down at his wife as she slept. Zoey would wake soon to head to the bakery. He'd gotten a couple hours sleep last night, but not much. Something was off with Zoey. He couldn't put his finger on it, but something was different. It was a feeling he had when he was near her. She just wasn't the same.

Slade knew Zoey worried that the black magic that had tried to kill her was still inside of her. He hoped it wasn't that. However, he couldn't be sure. So he planned to ask Galen to look at her. Zoey would throw a fit, but in the end she'd know it was for the best. Slade would do anything for her, even if it meant tossing her over his shoulder and taking her to the doctor.

"I can feel you staring at me."

"Can you feel me kissing you?" Slade asked a moment before he placed his lips on hers. Yes, he'd do anything for her.

. . .

Zoey knew it was coming. She was mixing muffins, just waiting to be scared out of her mind.

"Hey."

Even knowing Jane was popping in, it still surprised her when her friend appeared.

"Morning, Jane," Zoey said, pretending she hadn't jumped a little in surprise. "Are you feeling any better?"

Jane sighed and grabbed a chocolate chip muffin that had just come out of the oven. "I feel off. I didn't sleep well."

Zoey stopped and turned to look at Jane. She looked off. "Do witches get sick?"

"I don't think so. We're healers. We can get injured, but I've never heard of a witch getting so much as a cold before. Why?" Jane asked.

"I'm feeling off myself. I thought it was the black magic still inside me. Do you think it could be in you too?" Zoey asked.

"Right now, I think anything is possible," Jane said before biting into the muffin. "But this makes it all better."

Zoey smiled as she whipped up another batch.

"Please tell me you're making chocolate chip muffins."

Oh Goddess. Zoey jumped again as Agnes suddenly appeared with Vilma. She had to stop being surprised like that.

"For you, anything," Zoey said, giving them each a smile.

Agnes and Vilma looked between her and then Jane.

"Something is different," Vilma said slowly.

"We're not feeling right," Jane said between bites. "Maybe you know. Do witches get colds?"

"Usually our bodies can fight off anything as trivial as that. Now, being spelled, having our powers stripped, being physically injured . . . that's a different story," Vilma told them.

"Who's sick?" Lauren asked and Zoey praised herself for not jumping this time.

"They're off. Look at them," Agnes said as she pointed to Jane and Zoey.

"Witches don't get sick." Even as Lauren said it, she placed the back of her hand to Zoey's forehead. "No fever. Have Galen look at you two. I'm more worried about black magic infecting you both."

"Yes, Grand Mistress," Jane answered for her and Zoey.

Zoey grumbled to herself. She didn't want to go to the doctor. "Agnes, can you and Vilma get the front ready to open?"

"Done!" they called out a second later. Magic was a wonderful thing. It meant you never had to clean.

"Thank you. Go ahead and flip the sign and unlock the door." Zoey carried out tray after tray of breakfast pastries. She knew after yesterday the place would be packed. The bakery had turned into the town's morning gossip hub.

Zoey's head was in the display case when the bell tinkled over the door. It didn't ring again since so many people were waiting to get in and talk. The line was out the door. Jane jumped in and helped fill orders as Zoey ran the register. Witches and humans alike couldn't stop talking about the fire at the distillery.

Zoey knew the second Slade entered the bakery. She felt him before she saw him. When she looked up, he smiled at her, and she felt that all was right in her world once again.

"Good morning, sweetness. Do you need any help?"

"Yes, you can help restock this display if you don't mind," Zoey said as Slade moved around the back of the counter and placed a lingering kiss to her lips.

Zoey was filled with love. She smiled and then everything went to hell.

Screams echoed through the small town. The people in line shoved their way farther inside the bakery. Zoey looked to Slade and saw the worry in her eyes reflected in his. Together they pushed through the panicked crowd to get to the glass door.

"Oh my Goddess," Zoey said under her breath.

Snakes covered Moonshine Hollow. They filled the street. They writhed on the sidewalk. They hung from the light posts and from the sides of the buildings.

"I've got this," Polly whispered as she snuck out the back. A second later an owl came swooping down. Its talons dug into a snake trying to climb the front door of the bakery.

Hawks and owls joined, but there were simply too many snakes.

"We have to do something," Lauren said.

Zoey could only nod. It felt as if the black magic had a grasp on her throat and was slowly squeezing.

"It's the black magic, isn't it?" Slade asked. "It's still affecting you."

Zoey nodded and Slade wasted no time. He pulled her back into the kitchen and then they were gone. When Zoey opened her eyes, she was in Scotland and Galen was staring at them with surprise.

"Moonshine Hollow is under attack by snakes and Zoey's choking again."

"Not choking," Zoey said.

Galen had his hands on her and was already motioning for her to open her mouth. "Nothing. I don't feel black magic in you. I think it is ordinary fear. Something is different though."

"But I'm not infected and I'm not sick?" Zoey asked.

Galen shook his head. "No."

"Good. I can handle fear." Zoey grabbed him and in a flash they were back in Moonshine Hollow.

The screaming hadn't stopped. Now the screams of the humans mixed with the screams of the witches who could shift into hawks. "Galen, do you feel black magic?" Zoey asked.

"Yes. It's very strong," Galen confirmed as they shoved their way into the bakery.

This time Zoey recognized her fear and faced it head-on. The choking feeling lessened even as Zoey saw the snakes growing. They were getting bigger and they were multiplying. Windows were being broken and snakes were slithering their way inside the buildings along Main Street.

"There's no choice. We have to use our magic," Zoey said, feeling the black magic pushing against her body, searching for any sign of weakness. She refused to give it any. Not this time.

"I agree," Jane said, appearing by her side. "Polly is leading them on coordinated attacks to keep them from getting into the bakery. Most of the residents have packed themselves inside. But Polly and the other shifters can't keep the snakes at bay long."

"Out the back," Zoey ordered as a herd of cats joined the battle.

Zoey heard the people gasping in shock and disbelief. Tears of fear mixed with disbelief at the animals outside the door from them.

"Look, it's that black cat I saw last year," Nancy said, "the one with teal eyes". She was a townsperson who loved to adopt stray animals and had tried to adopt Grand Mistress Lauren when she was stuck in cat form.

Zoey motioned for the witches in the room to follow.

Slowly they made their way into the kitchen. "We're going to use our powers, but we need to hide," Zoey whispered.

"It's not perfect, but I can make an ivy shield. They'll see it and our powers, but they won't see who is behind it," Vilma suggested.

"I can help, Vilma," Jane said as she reached for Galen's hand.

"I don't see the problem with snakes," Neferu said with a roll of her eyes. Neferu was from the Egyptian time and had been friends with Nefertiti and Cleopatra.

"They're black magic snakes," Slade reminded her.

Neferu wrinkled her nose in distaste. "Poor things. Giving snakes a bad name. Let's round them up. Come on, Galen. You'll be needed."

12

"Neferu, I'll take the far end and send them to you," Agnes said.

"Got it." Neferu flexed her fingers, ready for action.

Zoey and her group went out the back door and with a flick of her fingers, the snakes in front of her disappeared into nothingness. She was the fifth element. Where others were bound by the four elements–Earth, Air, Fire, and Water—Zoey had what some called Quintessence, the fifth and highest element responsible for nature and the substance that made up the celestial bodies. It was a white light that would simply make whatever she aimed it at disappear into nothingness.

Agnes *poofed* away. Zoey shot the snakes with white light as Slade burned them with his fire power to give them a snake-free area to set up the ivy wall. When they were snake free and hiding behind the brick exterior wall of the bakery, Vilma and Jane worked together to build a wall of ivy with small slits in it to look through for Neferu, Zoey, and Slade.

Zoey and her group walked out from the side of the building and behind the massive wall of ivy. She heard the leaves rustling as snakes began to crawl around the bottom of the ivy.

"What exactly is Agnes going to do?" Zoey asked Neferu as they got into position.

"That," Neferu said with a smile. "I forgot how much pizzazz Agnes really has with her powers."

Zoey leaned forward and looked through the small window in the ivy hiding their identity. There was no way around showing their powers, but they could at least try to protect themselves from Witch Trials 2.0.

"Oh my Goddess," Zoey whispered in equal parts awe and disbelief. "Do I see a Bluetick Coonhound being ridden by . . . is that Davy Crockett?"

Neferu smiled and Zoey did a double take. Neferu was always so serious. Although how could anyone not smile at a wall of water shaped like Davy Crockett riding a coonhound? Davy's watery figure reached out and grabbed snakes off the buildings as the coonhound ate the ones on the street.

"I guess I'm up," Neferu said as she aimed her hands at the water. Right before it would have crashed down onto them, light blue light shot from Neferu's fingers. Her long black hair blew in the wind she created. The air power shot forward and whipped around and around Davy and the dog until the figures slowly disbursed into a funnel of water. "Your turn," Neferu said to Zoey and Galen.

Zoey aimed her powers at the tornado-like funnel and let her white light fly at the same time Galen chanted in the old language to purge the area of black magic. Zoey's energy swirled around the funnel and then there was nothing. The water and the snakes were simply gone. Main Street was as clean as the morning after a rain. Windows sparkled, and with a flick of Vilma's green powers, flowers along Main Street rose up in their pots and had never looked better.

"We better get back into the bakery and pretend we were there the whole time," Jane said. They all *poofed* into the bakery's kitchen and walked out together. Zoey and her witches stood there as if they'd been watching from the back of the room the whole time as people talked about the wall of water and the snakes.

"Was something in the muffins?" Peach asked as she turned to find Zoey. "Because I can't possibly have seen what I thought I did."

Zoey blinked not knowing how to handle this.

"The nutmeg in the rye muffins," Vilma said as if suddenly having an epiphany.

"What?" Zoey asked as several older people began to nod.

"Oh, honey," Peach said with a tsk. "Too much nutmeg can cause hallucinations."

"So can the rye if ergot fungus was in it," Agnes said with a "that's what it is" nod of her head. "Did you know some believe the people of Salem ate ergot fungus infected rye and that's what caused the witch trials?"

"Oh my Goddess," Zoey muttered in disbelief.

Peach turned to Fay and they both laughed. "The Moonshine Hollow Witch Trials all because we ate some tainted rye . . . can you imagine?" Peach asked with a laugh.

"Even high on nutmeg and fungus I can't believe in witches. Can you imagine pointy- hatted, broom-wielding, ugly warty-nosed witches hanging out in Moonshine Hollow?" Clara giggled.

"Well," Zoey said with a forced laugh. "No more nutmeg and rye!"

"I thought I was eating a chocolate chip muffin," Clara

said. Zoey wiggled her finger as Clara looked down. "Oh, nope. It's rye."

"I thought I ordered chocolate chip too. I never knew rye and nutmeg could taste so good," Maribelle said, sending Zoey a smile. "Just to be sure, though, Davy Crockett didn't ride Smokey, Tennessee's mascot dog, down Main Street to drown all the snakes and then disappear into thin air?" Maribelle asked. Zoey gave a little nervous laugh. Maribelle began to laugh too. "That does sound crazy. Wow, never make these muffins again."

"If you all come to the clinic, Dr. Galen and I can give you something to counter the hallucinations," Lauren called out. "Put a rye muffin in everyone's hands now," Lauren whispered to Zoey.

It took a moment to concentrate, but she got a muffin in every hand of every person along Main Street, even if they weren't in the bakery.

"Remind them I did deliveries this morning to anyone who wasn't here," Zoey whispered back to Lauren.

"Will do. You all did a good job. However, we've now had three attacks in less than forty-eight hours. Whoever is behind this isn't giving us the time we need to solve the mystery. Be prepared for anything."

"Yes, Grand Mistress," Zoey said, letting out a long breath. What was going on? Why was she feeling so off? Why was fear creeping into her heart?

Slade looked around the clearing at all the witches gathered. They were all talking about the black magic. Slade could sense the fear. They'd all lived through the attack at court when Alexander turned on them and they were afraid it was happening again. He didn't blame them for their fear.

He wondered the same thing. Was Alexander somehow behind this? But he couldn't be. Slade had watched both Alexander and Ian die.

"They're guessing about witches now. What are we going to do?" Fern asked nervously. "Should we leave and go into hiding again?"

"No," Slade said suddenly and much harsher than he intended. "This is our home. We ran and hid before. Never again."

"I agree with my son," Magnus said as he came to stand next to Slade.

Slade had never told Magnus what it meant that he'd welcomed Slade into his family so readily. After Slade's father, Alexander, murdered Slade's mother, Helena, he had no family left. Grand Master Linus had been the father Slade needed until he was killed last year. Magnus had filled that role as if by an unspoken agreement between himself and Linus since Linus went to the Goddess. However, it wasn't just Magnus. Zoey's human mother and stepfather had also welcomed him into their family. Bradley taught Slade how to golf. Slade didn't tell him he'd golfed St. Andrews two hundred years ago. But even Slade could admit that after two hundred years he was a little rusty swinging the clubs. The thing was, he had a family now. He had a town he was a part of. He had a wife he loved and who was loved by this town. He wasn't going to run. Not anymore.

"We need to fight. The time has come. If you're not willing to fight for the freedom we've enjoyed this past year, you can leave now. But those who stay know you're going to fight," Magnus declared. A few people looked around and then *poofed* away, but not many.

"I will fight," Samuel said, stepping forward.

"I will fight," Polly said, reaching for her husband's hand.

Slade watched as witch after witch stepped forward and made their pledge.

"Then I turn the training over to Master Slade," Magnus told them.

"Polly, Samuel, will you help?" Slade asked.

"Of course." Samuel inclined his head to Slade in a sign of respect.

"Then let's break into three groups and get started."

Slade glanced at his wife, who was deep in discussion with Galen. "Jane, Zoey, Galen," Slade called out. They walked over to him with question in their eyes. "I want you three to work on uncovering the powers Galen has."

"Good idea," Jane said, turning to her husband. "Let's get to work."

13

Polly was exhausted. She'd worked with the Claritase on fighting skills for three hours. She was used to working long hours, but all she could think about was taking a nap. The trouble was, evil didn't wait while you rested.

"I'm worried about you," Samuel said quietly as he joined her on the couch.

"Me? Why?" Polly asked as she snuggled her head against her husband's shoulder.

"You seem off today."

"I'm just tired. The stress of this is starting to affect me. I wish whoever was behind this would just step forward and fight us head-on. Instead, they are hiding in the shadows and having fun with these menacing attacks." Just thinking about it made Polly mad.

"He, she, them . . . whoever it is, will have their reckoning." Samuel kissed the top of her head. "Rest up. Tonight is the town meeting in the park to talk about what to do about the distillery. Slade wants us there to protect the people in case anything happens."

"That's right. It's a potluck. I signed us up to bring

something." Polly yawned. The last think she saw before she closed her eyes was Samuel's concerned gaze.

Samuel walked into the police station to find Slade behind his desk. He looked exhausted too. "Everything okay?" he asked his best friend.

"I think I've lost my voice from all the phone calls I have fielded this afternoon over the snakes and the drugged muffins."

"It was quick thinking. I hope it doesn't hurt Zoey's business. She shouldn't have to take the hit for someone trying to mess with the town."

Slade sighed and leaned back in his chair. "She's worried about that and it's all wearing on her. Zoey almost fell asleep helping Neferu, Niles, Fern, and Raiden look through millenniums worth of records, personal journals, and whatever else they can find."

"Polly is wiped too. I left her sleeping on the couch." Samuel paused and thought about the records. "No luck finding a link between the six of us?" Samuel asked.

Slade shook his head. "We're all True Loves. There's some minor connections here and there, but we thought we'd find something that changed everything we knew."

"Maybe it's not that big. Maybe it is just friendship?"

"It could be, but is friendship stronger than True Love?" Slade asked. "I mean, I love you, bro, but not nearly as much as my wife."

Samuel chuckled. "Feeling's mutual. Who do you think is behind this and why are they going after the town? They aren't hurting us witches."

"I've wondered about that too. Maybe they aren't as

strong as we think so they go after the weak?" Slade
shrugged and then ran his hand over his face as he thought.

"Black magic does show a weakness in character. It's a
bully. They're picking on those who can't fight back."

Slade leaned forward and put his elbows on the desk.
"Do you think they're trying to expose us on purpose?"

Samuel thought about it. It wasn't a bad idea. "The
caskets made us use magic in the open. The fire did so on an
even bigger scale. Then the snakes . . . you could be right."

"They want a second Salem," Slade said, warming to the
idea.

"What happens if we are exposed?" Samuel asked. As
crazy as this sounded, it made more sense than anything
else. Revenge was always a motive, but why involve the town
then?

"I honestly don't know," Slade admitted. "But if things
continue as they have been, I'm afraid we'll find out soon
enough."

Zoey stood beside Maribelle, Polly, Jane, and Grand
Mistress Lauren as they waited for Mr. Earnest to arrive at
the park named after his family. Zoey shifted uncomfortably
as she looked to her left at Earnest Creek, which really was a
small river. It was there she had killed Ian. It was there her
father made a stand against whoever was wielding the black
magic. He'd been able to hold it off until they all could
escape, but he couldn't completely defeat it.

Zoey looked to the right slightly behind the stage that
had been used for everything from theater to beauty
pageants to the announcing of the Moonshine Flavor of the

Year. Up in the mountain behind it was where Grand Master Linus had received his fatal wound.

Yet, you'd never know it. The leaves were vibrant in shades of orange, yellow, and red. The air held the smell of fall, yet still had the last strains of summer's warmth. Moonshine Hollow was simply the most beautiful and relaxing place Zoey knew. It was no wonder that witches, who derived their power from the elements, were so happy there. Now, if only it would last.

Zoey saw Slade and Samuel step up on the stage. She looked around and saw witches fanning out to form a protective circle around the humans who had become their friends over the past year. Agnes and Vilma stood with every member of the Iris and Opossum clubs. Neferu stood near them as well. The younger looking witches were with the Mountaineers, the club for the younger generation in town. Most were single and some were newlyweds like Maribelle and Dale. Finally, Mr. Earnest stepped up onto the stage.

Slade stepped forward and the crowd quieted down. "The burning of the distillery was an intentional act. There was an accelerant used. We have witness reports and—"

Slade stopped and Zoey watched as he looked down at his hand and then up to the sky.

Zoey held out her hands, palm up to feel for rain.

Splat.

The rain was red. The rain was blood. Evil was here.

Maribelle screamed as the red drops fell on her hands. She wasn't the only one. Women screamed with fear, men cursed in disbelief, and Zoey was already turning to put herself between Maribelle and whatever threat was coming.

"Into position! Defend the town!" Zoey yelled, shoving Maribelle toward the inner circle that hadn't been there seconds before. Witches now all turned to face any threat to the town as they moved the town to the center space between them.

"Zoey," Grand Mistress said softly, "once we do this, there's no turning back."

Thunder shook the hollow. Red lightning streaked across the sky and exploded onto the earth near the citizens. The clouds opened and blood rain fell in heavy sheets, drenching the people and hiding their screams under the claps of thunder and crashing lightning strikes.

"We don't have a choice," Zoey yelled over the noise of the blood storm and the terrified screams of her town.

"No, we don't. Look!" Lauren yelled as she pointed at the creek.

Zoey looked through the thick rain. She felt it before she saw it. The shaking of the earth and the near deafening sound of water rushing forward was a sound she'd never forget. Her father hadn't been able to defeat it last time. He'd only been able to hold it off for a short time while they transported. Not this time though. There were too many townspeople to transport and Zoey sure wasn't going to leave anyone behind.

"Zoey!" Maribelle cried as she clutched at her husband's arm. Her eyes were wide with fear as she reached for Zoey, hoping to protect her friend.

"I won't let it hurt you," Zoey swore. Maribelle's forehead creased in confusion as blood ran off the tip of her nose and down her face.

"This is what we've been training for!" Slade yelled. "Protect the town!"

14

Witches closed ranks, forcing the townspeople to stand shoulder to shoulder inside the circle of protectors. Some people panicked and tried to run, but they were rounded up and held in the tight circle as the witches worked them closer and closer together.

"The Six with me!" Slade yelled as he transported from the stage and reappeared next to Zoey. Some of the townspeople saw it and Zoey heard the gasps, but she couldn't worry about that now.

They stood together—Slade, Zoey, Samuel, Polly, Galen, and Jane. Ten feet behind them stood Magnus, Lauren, Agnes, Vilma, Neferu, Fern, Niles, and Raiden. Ten feet behind the council, the witches of the Tenebris and Claritase had joined hands completely encircling the townspeople.

"Shield!" Zoey heard Lauren yell as the tsunami of blood water came into view. It was easily a hundred feet high. Screams of fear and cries of terror came from the townspeople.

Zoey heard Maribelle yelling for her a second before the

darkness from the clouds was turned to light. Green, dark blue, light blue, and red energy filled the space behind Zoey. The screams were silenced in shock as a dome of power rose up from the ground to protect the people.

The tsunami of blood ripped up trees and boulders as it rushed forward. Zoey grounded her feet and opened her senses. She felt menace and evil churning in the blood wave. Her powers reached for it, but Zoey pulled them back.

Instead, she pulled from the energy from the good around her. Her powers surged to her fingertips, but she held it there. She could feel its restlessness, its desire to take on the evil, but she forced her power to stay in her hands. Her energy grew as it churned, waiting to be released until her hands were nothing but white balls of light.

"Now!" Slade yelled.

Zoey lifted her hands with her friends and let her powers flow.

The battle between good and evil was on the moment Zoey's powers hit the towering wave. The black magic screamed in anger at her white magic. Shadows reached out from the wave as it tried to grab the energy of the Goddess. Zoey was shoved back a step from the power of it. She felt the black magic trying to steal her power. The dark magic slithered along the energy path heading toward her fingers as Zoey struggled to push it back.

"No!" she heard Jane scream.

Zoey spared a glance and saw her friend on her knees as her green earth power darkened from the black magic. Galen grabbed his wife and pushed her behind him. He raised his own hands and a blinding light shot forward as he chanted in the old language. This chant was different from the one at the cemetery, but whatever he was doing was working. The shadows shrieked and the wave slowed.

Jane was weakened but Agnes was there to pick her up. "Chant with your husband," Agnes ordered as Jane reached out and placed her hand on Galen's arm. She closed her eyes and Zoey could see her green energy seeping from her hand into Galen.

The chant started low, but then Jane was screaming it. Samuel picked up on the wording and joined as his air power grew stronger. Then Polly joined in with a fierceness Zoey never expected.

"Together," Slade said, reaching for Zoey.

He placed his hand on her shoulder and her energy took on a light purple color. Energy surged through her body. From behind, her power surged through her like a hurricane as her father placed his hand on her other shoulder. Eileen stepped forward and placed her hand on Jane's shoulder.

Samuel and Polly clasped hands, each holding a hand out to fight the darkness.

Zoey turned to Slade and then looked at the others. She could hear the humans' cries. She saw Maribelle and Dale trying to get to her to rescue her. She saw the witches all holding hands protecting the town. Together.

"We can't hold it much longer," Samuel yelled as they stood in the shadow of the tsunami. He was right. While power surged through her body, it wasn't enough to stop the wave that was now towering over them.

"Together, we need to be together!" Zoey screamed over the roar of the wave. She reached out and grabbed Samuel. The power surge rocked her on her feet as the wave began to crest. "We can't stop it but we can survive it. We have to be together. Get to the town circle!"

"Go!" her father yelled.

"Dad!" Zoey saw her father plant his feet. He tossed his

head back and screamed as he used all the energy he had. A blue, unlike any color any witch had, shot from his hands and into the blood wave.

"Go, Zoey! Protect the town," her father yelled to her.

Zoey was going to stay and fight, but Slade yanked her off her feet and ran with her even as she reached out for her father. The circle was temporarily broken as the witches made room for them. They locked hands and Zoey looked over her shoulder to see her father defending them as Samuel, Galen, Jane, and Polly chanted as loud as they could and encouraged everyone else to do so.

Her father dropped to his knees. His arms were shaking as the full weight of the wave crashed down on him.

"Dad!"

An explosion of power burst from her hands and traveled through the circle of witches as the blood wave pounded down on them. The energy of the dome darkened, but it didn't break. Not when her energy surge of white power rippled through the witches, hand to hand, around the circle and over the dome. Some witches cried out in pain as her powerful energy surged through them. Other's clenched their teeth and squeezed the hand next to them so hard it probably broke some bones. However, not a single witch broke the circle.

It sounded as if they were under an umbrella during a hail storm as the blood wave crashed and rolled around them. The townspeople ducked and covered their heads. Maribelle was crying as Dale held her protectively in his arms. His eyes rose and met Zoey's. She saw the confusion, the disbelief, but she also saw something else—compassion.

Tears came to Zoey's eyes as the wave crashed onto them in what felt like a never-ending assault. Trees, boulders, and blood hit against the dome from every angle.

"Chant!" Slade ordered her as he squeezed her hand tightly.

Zoey looked at her True Love and saw his lavender eyes glowing with the shared powers. Maribelle raised her head from Dale's chest. Her fearful eyes locked with Zoey's. "Save us, please."

Zoey didn't look away as tears ran down Maribelle's face. Slowly she began to chant. First it was The Six. Then the councils joined in. To her right and left, other witches began to pick up the chant. Like the wave at a sporting event, the chant began to circle its way around the witches until they all chanted as one. Their powers flared with new life. They intertwined, weaving a beautiful blanket of protection over them all. The sound of the pounding blood began to lessen as the chants grew louder.

Next to her, Galen began to glow stronger. This time it wasn't just his hands, but his whole body shone brightly. Zoey and Jane moved their hands from Galen's grasp up to each shoulder. Galen's hands shot upward. His head fell back as he let out a primal scream. The light was so blinding everyone closed their eyes and adverted their gaze. It was as if a nuclear bomb had gone off. The light turned brighter and brighter until it exploded into nothingness.

Zoey blinked her eyes open as Galen's shoulder fell away from her touch.

"Galen!" Jane yelled.

Zoey had to blink several times until things came into focus. When they did, she found Galen on the ground with blood trickling from his nose, ears, and even from his closed eyes. She also found that the wave of blood was gone. In its place, a trickle of blood ran harmlessly over the blood soaked grass.

It was over. They survived.

"Dad!"

Zoey pulled free from Slade's hold and turned around. Her father was gone.

"Galen? Can you hear me?" Jane screamed full of worry.

"We'll find him," Slade to Zoey. "But first we have multiple situations to deal with."

Zoey looked around as the witches dropped their hands and stepped back from the townspeople. Some of the witches collapsed. Some were shaking from the exertion. Others tried to stand strong and proud as they were greeted with nothing but silence from the town.

Lauren was rushing to Galen's side as Zoey finally moved into action and dropped to the bloody ground next to Galen.

"He's alive, but barely," Lauren said as she closed her eyes. She rubbed her hands together and sighed. "My power is too depleted."

"Jane, you have to break open your memory. Your True Love can save him but you need all your power to do so," Aunt Eileen said, joining them.

"We'll help you," Zoey said. She looked up at their group who rushed forward. Aunt Eileen held one of Jane's hand and Zoey held the other. Polly rubbed Jane's back as Slade and Samuel each placed a hand on her shoulder. "You're strong enough to break down any obstacle, Jane. Don't look for a way around. Smash your way through it," Lauren told her.

"What's going on?" Maribelle asked.

"Shh, dear," Agnes whispered. "Jane has to find the strength to break down the barrier holding her full powers back so that she can save Galen's life."

Maribelle was quiet and then took a step forward. She

dropped to her knees and placed a hand on Jane's arm. "We're here for you, Jane."

Zoey mouthed *thank you* to her friend and then closed her eyes. She focused what was left of her power, now nothing more than a trickle, to help Jane.

15

Jane looked down at Galen and felt a panic like no other. What if she couldn't save him? She couldn't lose him now. "Don't let negativity enter your thoughts or your heart. Darkness has no place here," Lauren whispered.

"Jane, look at your True Love. Look at the love of your friends and family. You are surrounded by love. Give it to Galen. Let him feel it," Zoey said gently but firmly.

Jane looked over at Aunt Eileen, Slade, Polly, and Samuel touching her one arm and Lauren, Zoey, and Maribelle gently touching her arm on her on one side. She felt Agnes, Vilma, Neferu, and Fern gently touching her back too.

"I don't know what to do, but I'm here for you Jane," Maribelle whispered.

"Think about goodness, love, and strength," Lauren whispered back. "You're very brave, Maribelle."

Jane's eyes teared as she looked at the people supporting her. Jane closed her eyes and went back into her memory. She didn't go gently. She didn't go slowly. She raced to the past. She saw the stone circle and Galen's grandmother talking to her father, but Jane didn't stop at the dense fog that followed that memory. She ran through it. She didn't slow. She sliced the fog with her hands, shooting her power into it as she pushed through.

The fog had taken on a heavy quality. It was trying to slow her down, but Jane refused to slow. She pushed harder and felt the waves of love and friendship from those touching her. It gave her the power to push through the darkness of her memories.

She started to see memories of her father cursing her mother. Memories of always being on the move. Memories of her father blaming her for his lack of a son. Memories of her father calling her mother's family traitors. Memories she wished she never had to remember. The pain, the loneliness, and the constant disappointment she felt from her father even as he tried to hide it when he looked at her so he could fake his way into an heir. Jane pushed past the teen years and now her legs were sluggish as the fog was as thick like waist-deep mud as she entered her childhood memories.

A scream of pain reached her ears, coming from her memory. She wouldn't stop, no matter how painful the memory was. Jane had to save Galen. The memory was hidden behind fog so thick she didn't know if she could make it through. Instead, she reached her hand for Zoey's and clasped her friend tightly. Zoey had very little power left, but it was enough to boost Jane through. The friendship and protection Zoey offered Jane fueled the positive memories that pushed the fog apart.

You worthless child! Jane's father yelled at her. Jane saw her father release his hand from Jane's head and shove her back.

Little Jane fell crying to the floor.

The great and powerful Kendrick family. What a farce. You are nothing but worthless wastes of space! her father ranted at her mother.

You swore to love her or there will be no more children, her mother snapped as she came to hug Jane protectively.

You have no power left. I thought you gave it to Jane, but all I feel is the Farrington power. While that is strong enough, she should have double that with the Farrington and the Kendrick blood flowing through her. Worthless. You both are weak chains hanging around my neck and preventing the Farrington line from its destiny!

Her father stormed from the memory. Her mother hugged little Jane tightly and began to rock her as she sang softly. *True power comes from True Love. Only when you find True Love will your true powers be shown. Through the darkness comes the light of your love. Follow the light from the thought of your love and there you'll find your powers.* Her mother sang the little song over and over until the memory faded.

Jane had been thinking of the wrong things. She'd been trying to make her way back to the memory of her mother and aunt hiding her powers, thinking that would be the key to unlocking them.

Jane stood in the fog of her memories and brought Galen to mind. She remembered their first meeting. She remembered their first kiss. She remembered the bond they shared. Jane smiled as she remembered the way their bond glowed and connected them, heart to heart, as soul mates.

Through the fog, a shimmer of gold appeared — Galen. It was their True Love bond. It started as a faint shimmer until Jane was following a gold rope past their first memories together, past their wedding, and through the past year of their love and life. Jane paused in her mind as up ahead she saw a glowing travel trunk.

Jane followed the golden light of their bond until it disappeared into the trunk. It looked old, like a chest from four hundred years ago. It was a rectangular wooden trunk with leather straps and an old lock. Jane reached down and pulled the lock open. She could feel a power unlike anything she'd felt before inside it. When she lifted the lid, green earth power surged free.

Open your heart. Jane heard her mother's voice say.

Jane thought of Galen, thought of their love, and opened her heart to the power. The green energy wrapped her in a warm hug. Jane swore she smelled and felt her mother in the energy. "I love you, Mom," Jane whispered with a tear in her eye to the power. It let go of Jane and surged into her heart.

Jane's eyes popped open. Maribelle was shaking her hand as if she'd been stung, but she wasn't crying or backing away. "You're glowing brighter," Zoey told her.

"You have the Kendrick power. Save your husband," Aunt Eileen said with a teary smile.

Jane listened as Grand Mistress Lauren told her how to use some of her power to save Galen's life. She felt his soul when she placed her hands on him. As she held him, she felt their bond surge back to life.

"Jane," Galen muttered. His eyes blinked open and Jane had never been so relieved. "You're glowing."

"I have my powers back," Jane said with a tearful smile.

"How did you find them?" Galen asked. He was alive and he was talking, but he wasn't making any effort to sit up.

"I found them by focusing on our love," Jane said, smiling down at him before looking at her aunt. "I don't understand. What I am feeling is my power times ten. I'm not Zoey level, but I feel pretty close to it."

Her aunt nodded at her. "You carry the power of the Kendricks."

"But don't you also have the Kendrick power? You're Eileen Kendrick, after all," Jane asked even as she could hear the citizens of Moonshine Hollow growing restless behind them.

"I am. But my sister Aurora was special. She was the firstborn and before our mother died, she bequeathed all of her power to her. It wasn't supposed to be done. In fact, it was a big no-no."

"It still is," Grand Mistress Lauren said flatly, crossing her arms over her chest.

"Why would she do that then? Grandmother was a council member, wasn't she?" Jane asked.

Her aunt nodded again. "Your grandfather had visions. I inherited some of that power, but not nearly as much as he had. However, he told your grandmother that their granddaughter's life depended on her getting that power. She never questioned why. She just did what she needed to do. Aurora was only a hundred years old when our mother died during the Viking invasion of England. She was captured when she tried to keep the peace. They tied her up and tortured her in front of the keep. They allowed her daughter to say goodbye before they burned her. Your grandmother transferred all her powers when your mother hugged her goodbye. No one knew of the transfer. Then your father came sniffing around a couple hundred years later. Everyone knew your mother had power, just no idea how much. She was very secretive about it. But there was no hiding the Kendrick power. You could practically smell it on her."

"So he wanted her because he wanted to steal her power," Jane said, thinking back to his anger when he couldn't steal Jane's power just as he wanted to steal her mother's.

"That's right," Aunt Eileen said sadly.

"The council will need to approve of your power transfer. That's two transfers you've received. Your grandmother's and your mother's. Now I understand at least," Grand Mistress Lauren said to her, and Jane began to panic.

"You're not going to take them, are you?"

Lauren was quiet as Jane clutched Galen's hand.

"I will vote for you to keep them," Zoey said, coming to her defense. "It's obvious her grandfather saw this moment in time in a vision. Jane is here for a reason and those powers were given to her for a reason."

"I'm inclined to agree. We'll still need to discuss and approve it at another time. Right now we have an audience," Lauren said.

"Is everyone safe?" Galen asked, finally sitting up and looking around.

It was then Jane realized not everyone was there. "Zoey, where is your father?"

Her best friend's eyes pooled with tears and all Zoey could manage was a slight shake of her head. She mouthed, "I don't know," as her voice failed her.

"He can't be dead," Grand Mistress Lauren said with her brow knit in confusion. "If he were, he could appear to us and he certainly would. He wouldn't be one to elect not to."

"Could he still be alive?" Zoey whispered with the first bloom of hope.

"We can help look for Magnus, right Dale?" Maribelle asked as the humans of Moonshine Hollow no longer stood quietly behind them, but were now surrounding them.

"Did we all have more of Zoey's trippy muffins?" Fay

asked slowly as she looked down at her blood covered hands.

"I might sound crazy, but are you super heroes up against a super villain?" Peach asked. "I know that sounds crazy, but I can't think of any rational way to explain what just happened."

"Oh my God! No, they're not super heroes. They're *witches!*" Clara gasped. "You'd made a joke about the witch trials, but that wasn't a joke. You're witches and you tried to kill us."

16

Zoey's eyes locked onto her friend's frantic ones. Clara looked on the brink of hysteria. Zoey stood up, her legs wobbled, but then Slade was there on one side and Maribelle on the other.

"Don't be ridiculous, Clara," Maribelle snapped. "They didn't try to kill us. They protected us."

"Then what was that giant red wave? This is blood isn't it? Were you all sacrificing us?" Clara's voice echoed around the clearing as more people in the crowd became agitated. "You notice they're not denying that they are witches."

Zoey stood with her husband and her best friend by her side. Slowly the park divided. Witches stood behind Zoey and humans stood behind Clara. Maribelle and Dale were the exception.

"I'm not denying it because," Zoey said, holding up her hand to quiet the crowd, "we are witches."

Zoey flinched at some of the reactions she got. Suddenly the flame of a witch burning didn't seem out of the question.

"Quiet!" Maribelle yelled. "We will hear them out. They

saved us from that wave of blood. Give Zoey time to answer it."

Agnes stepped forward with Vilma by her side. "It's not her story to tell. At least not yet. We were the first witches to arrive in Moonshine Hollow."

"Is that how you won moonshine recipe of the year? Did you use your magic?" Otis asked as all the Opossum men started to grumble.

"No. We don't use magic for that. In fact, we didn't use much magic at all until we were hunted down a year ago," Agnes said.

"Hunted?" Peach asked.

Agnes and Vilma nodded. Then Agnes stepped forward just a little bit. "It all started with the Goddess."

"Told you God was a woman," Peach said to her husband, Otis, who rolled his eyes.

The crowd was quiet as Agnes told the history of the Claritase and the Tenebris. She told of their purpose to help Earth and humans. She told about the attack. She told them about the deaths, whole families lost to the attack and then to the Hunters. She told them about being in hiding for four hundred years until Zoey came to Moonshine Hollow.

Zoey cringed as people laughed at how she accidentally inhaled a Tenebris Hunter. Then they sighed as they heard the truth of her and Slade's love story and her reunion with her father, whom everyone had believed dead for years. Agnes told them a shortened version of things, but with enough details for them to understand the battle they were in.

Zoey saw the disbelief. She saw the confusion. She saw the fear. However, she also saw the acceptance.

"What's stopping you from stealing the children and killing us all?" Clara asked.

"We'd never do that. We protect the innocent," Neferu said in her trademark haughtiness that shut Clara up.

"Wait," Ada Mae said. She was easily eighty years old and was a longtime member of the Iris Women's Group. "Six years ago, I burned my arm severely while baking. Do you all remember that?"

Several ladies from the group nodded.

"Vilma gave me a cream for the burn. It was gone an hour later. That was magic, wasn't it?"

"We were hiding and using magic put us in danger, but I couldn't see my friend suffer," Vilma admitted with a gentle smile.

"My broken leg?" Bart asked.

"I fixed that one," Agnes said, raising her hand.

"My son was very sick when he was born . . ."

"That was me," Vilma said, raising her hand.

Zoey watched as townsperson after townsperson asked if magic had been used on them.

"So, you're saying you helped all of us even though whenever you used magic it put you on the radar of these Hunters?" Fay finally asked.

Agnes and Vilma nodded.

"But what else have you done to us that we don't even know about?" Clara practically shrieked.

"Child, you need to calm down," Doris Bleacher, the very stern clinic secretary, snapped at Clara. "Lauren here has helped countless patients since she started at the clinic."

Zoey was shocked that mean Doris had come to their defense. She'd thought Doris would be the one to light the match to toss on the pyre.

"What about our Matthew? Why didn't you save him?" Hailey and Jacob Cohen asked of their son who had died at the hands of an evil witch, most likely the same one they were fighting now.

Zoey stopped Agnes from answering and stepped forward. Hailey turned tearful eyes to her, waiting for a reason they didn't save their little boy. "I failed. I was so new I didn't know I needed to protect the entire town. I thought only we witches were in danger. Matthew woke me up after he died. He needed me to find you and tell you he was sorry for playing in the creek when he shouldn't be."

"You and Slade visited us one night, right when it happened," Jacob said slowly.

"Matthew was with you, wasn't he? I felt him. I know I felt him." Hailey burst into tears and her husband hugged her close to him.

"He was," Slade answered for Zoey, thank Goddess because Zoey was crying too hard to speak. "He helped us learn evil was here. He saved so many of our lives. I'm sorry we couldn't save him. When we visited that night, he heard you tell us that you weren't mad at him and then he hugged you."

"I knew it. I knew we felt him!" Hailey was sobbing as tears ran down her husband's face and most cheeks of the town too. "But then I didn't feel him again. What happened to him?"

"Matthew was able to move on knowing you forgave him for going to the creek and that you loved him," Slade told them.

"Move on?" Jacob asked as he wiped the tears from his face.

"He's with his grandpappy," Zoey said quietly. She still remembered the boy's excited cheer as he ran into the afterlife.

Jacob sucked in a breath. "That's what Matthew called

my father. He died six months before Matthew. They were very close."

Suddenly Hailey launched herself at Zoey. With everything going on, Zoey didn't know whether to be afraid or not. Hailey wrapped her arms around her and sobbed into Zoey's neck. "Thank you. Thank you so much for telling us."

"What are you doing? They killed your child!" Clara yelled.

Hailey rounded on her and pointed her finger right in Clara's face. "No, they did not! The evil that made that blood wave and tried to kill us all tonight is what killed my son. Zoey and Slade made sure Matthew's soul was loved and gave us peace knowing he's with his grandfather in the afterlife."

"Can I ask a question?" Nancy asked, raising her hand.

"Of course," Zoey said, but Nancy wasn't looking at her. She was looking at Lauren.

"Do you, by any chance, turn into a cat?" Nancy asked.

Lauren smiled then and nodded. "Yes. I do. You were always very kind to me when I was in cat form."

"Wait," Billy Ray, the bartender at the Opossum Club, said, "all those birds and cats around town . . . the snakes! It wasn't the muffins, was it?"

"No, it wasn't the muffins," Lauren answered. "Some of us can shape shift into animals. Usually cats or birds."

"The evil behind the snakes is the same evil behind the blood wave and also behind the caskets and the distillery burning down," Slade told them.

Well, if you wanted the town to be on your side that did it. Zoey watched as the town turned all its anger on this unknown entity. They were ready to hunt it down themselves, whatever it was.

"I want to hunt them down more than anyone," Mr. Earnest said. "But you said you gave us new memories after some dealings with the bad guys last year. Will you do that now? Will you just erase our memory?"

Lauren smiled kindly at the crowd. "We're at your mercy. We will do whatever you want us to do. If you want to forget all about us, we can do that. If you want us to leave Moonshine Hollow and never come back, we can do that too. Or," she said, keeping all the attention on her as she raised a third finger. "Or we can stay here and live how we have been living this past year, except now you'll know what and who we really are. We only ask, for our safety, that the truth of who we are never leaves Moonshine Hollow."

"Because you're afraid of a modern witch trial?" Mr. Earnest asked.

All the witches nodded.

"We are here to help. We can't make everything perfect. We can't always prevent you from dying. But we can heal a broken bone and we can provide any support we are able to. This is the first time in our very long history that humans know who we are. We are trusting you with our lives and with our secrets. Imagine if word got out what we could do," Lauren said softly.

Dale grunted. "The government would take you away."

Billy Ray nodded. "Private companies would do medical research on you against your will."

"It would be horrible and cruel and I won't let it happen," Maribelle said as she grabbed Zoey's hand.

Mr. Earnest nodded and turned to the town. "We've had a really long day. Let's go home and get some rest. Tomorrow we will meet, privately," he said, glancing at the witches, "to discuss what course of action we want to take."

"That's very reasonable. We await your decision.

However, I must be honest. If you chose to let us stay, you could be in danger again. Whoever this evil force is, I can't promise they'll leave if we do. However, I can guarantee they won't leave if we stay. Either way, if we stay or leave, we will do everything we can to keep you safe and to end this war as fast as possible," Lauren said with a bow of her head to show respect.

The humans began to slowly leave the park. Some stopped to talk to their witch friends and to ask them some questions. By unspoken rule, none of the witches left the area. The night moon was dark in the sky and the park was eerily quiet after the humans all left.

"What do we do about them?" Neferu asked.

"We wait and see what they decide. We'll give them a choice to be a part of this war or not. Whatever they decide, we will survive. The Claritase are done hiding," Lauren said passionately.

Samuel turned to Slade and knelt down. "Grand Master Slade."

Zoey knew it was necessary. Her father was missing, maybe even dead. The Tenebris needed a leader. Her father had appointed him successor and the Tenebris had voted Slade as that leader.

"Only until we find my father-in-law," Slade said to the group. The Tenebris bowed their head in recognition of his leadership. "We need to find Magnus," Slade ordered.

Lauren came to stand next to Slade in a show of unity between the grand master and grand mistress. "Break off into pairs and search downriver," Lauren told the witches.

"Grab a healing drink on your way!" Agnes called out as she and Vilma whipped up their magical drinks to help the witches replenish their powers.

"You know I don't want to be grand master," Slade whispered to Zoey as he handed her a drink.

"I know, but you are until we figure out if my father is alive or—" Zoey couldn't say it.

"Or dead," Slade said quietly as he looked out over the park.

It seemed like forever as they all searched the woods. Some of the witches shifted so they could fly over the park and down water to search for Magnus. They spent most of the night searching only to come up empty. Magnus Rode was nowhere to be found.

Zoey looked back at the park as Slade led her home after a full night of searching. She struggled to leave, but she knew he was no longer here. She couldn't feel him.

"He's not dead," Slade said with a sureness Zoey wished she could feel.

"What do I do, Slade? Everything we've built here is about to fall apart." Zoey leaned against his side as Slade put his arm protectively around her.

"We're going to fight," Slade answered.

And so they were. The battle might be over, but the war was far from done. Zoey's energy sparked to life inside her. Deeper, darker, and bent for revenge. Whoever was behind this was going to pay.

Bluegrass Series

Bluegrass State of Mind

Risky Shot

Dead Heat

Bluegrass Brothers

Bluegrass Undercover

Rising Storm

Secret Santa: A Bluegrass Series Novella

Acquiring Trouble

Relentless Pursuit

Secrets Collide

Final Vow

Bluegrass Singles

All Hung Up

Bluegrass Dawn

The Perfect Gift

The Keeneston Roses

Forever Bluegrass Series

Forever Entangled

Forever Hidden

Forever Betrayed

Forever Driven

Forever Secret

Forever Surprised

Forever Concealed

Forever Devoted

Forever Hunted

Forever Guarded

Forever Notorious

Forever Ventured

Forever Freed

Forever Saved

Forever Bold

Forever Thrown

Forever Lies (coming Jan/Feb 2022)

Shadows Landing Series

Saving Shadows

Sunken Shadows

Lasting Shadows

Fierce Shadows

Broken Shadows

Framed Shadows

Endless Shadows

Fading Shadows (coming April/May 2022)

Women of Power Series

Chosen for Power

Built for Power

Fashioned for Power

Destined for Power

Web of Lies Series

Whispered Lies

Rogue Lies

Shattered Lies

Moonshine Hollow Series

Moonshine & Murder

Moonshine & Malice

Moonshine & Mayhem

Moonshine & Mischief

Moonshine & Menace

Moonshine & Masquerades (coming Dec 2021)

ABOUT THE AUTHOR

Kathleen Brooks is a New York Times, Wall Street Journal, and USA Today bestselling author. Kathleen's stories are romantic suspense featuring strong female heroines, humor, and happily-ever-afters. Her Bluegrass Series and follow-up Bluegrass Brothers Series feature small town charm with quirky characters that have captured the hearts of readers around the world.

Kathleen is an animal lover who supports rescue organizations and other non-profit organizations such as Friends and Vets Helping Pets whose goals are to protect and save our four-legged family members.

Email Notice of New Releases

https://kathleen-brooks.com/new-release-notifications

Kathleen's Website
www.kathleen-brooks.com
Facebook Page
www.facebook.com/KathleenBrooksAuthor
Twitter
www.twitter.com/BluegrassBrooks
Goodreads
www.goodreads.com

Made in United States
Orlando, FL
20 February 2022

15000952R10075